I couldn't believe it. My dad couldn't do this to me. Not on my first day in a new school. But it was him all right. You just can't mistake a beat-up half-ton with *Josh Morgan—Rodeo Clown* painted across the door. Especially when it's parked in the lane marked *School Buses Only*, and the principal himself is out there yelling at the driver.

I wished I could just disappear. I did take one step in the opposite direction, but I knew that was only prolonging the agony. There was only one thing to do. Get in the truck and get Dad out of there. I jumped in and slammed the door.

"Let's go, Dad," I said through my teeth, trying to keep the anger out of my voice.

Dad didn't even hear me. He was still yelling out the window at the principal. "I don't care if you are Mr. Whoever-You-Said. I'm Josh Morgan, and nobody pushes me around. If you don't believe that, why don't you take off your coat and that ugly purple necktie and we'll go a round right here and . . ."

I grabbed his arm. "Dad! Come on . . ."

He swung around in the seat and glared at me, his eyes blazing blue fire, and I thought he was going to hit me. He didn't, though. He just slammed the Ford into gear and burned out of there.

MARILYN HALVORSON is a full-time teacher who also runs a cattle ranch in Alberta, Canada. *Cowboys Don't Cry*, the winner of the Clarke Irwin/Alberta Culture Writing for Youth Competition, is her first novel for young adults.

ALSO AVAILABLE IN LAUREL-LEAF BOOKS:

Cowboys
Don't Cry

Marilyn Halvorson

LAUREL-LEAF BOOKS bring together under a single imprint outstanding works of fiction and nonfiction particularly suitable for young adult readers, both in and out of the classroom. Charles F. Reasoner, Professor Emeritus of Children's Literature and Reading, New York University, is consultant to this series.

Published by
Dell Publishing Co., Inc.
1 Dag Hammarskjold Plaza
New York, New York 10017

This work was first published in Canada by Irwin Publishing Inc.

Laurel-Leaf Library ® TM 766734, Dell Publishing Co., Inc.

ISBN: 0-440-91303-9

RL: 4.9

Reprinted by arrangement with Delacorte Press

Printed in the United States of America

December 1986

10 9 8 7 6 5 4 3 2 1

WFH

to Mom and Gale
and, especially, to
all the great kids in Sundre

Cowboys
Don't Cry

1

I couldn't believe it. My dad couldn't do this to me. Not on my first day in a new school. But it was him all right. You just can't mistake a beat-up half-ton with *Josh Morgan —Rodeo Clown* painted across the door. Especially when it's parked in the lane marked *School Buses Only,* and the principal himself is out there yelling at the driver.

I wished I could just disappear. I did take one step in the opposite direction, but I knew that was only prolonging the agony. There was only one thing to do. Get in the truck and get Dad out of there. I jumped in and slammed the door.

"Let's go, Dad," I said through my teeth, trying to keep the anger out of my voice.

Dad didn't even hear me. He was still yelling out the window at the principal. "I don't care if you are Mr. Whoever-You-Said. I'm Josh Morgan, and nobody pushes me around. If you don't believe that, why don't you take off your coat and that ugly purple necktie and we'll go a round right here and . . ."

I grabbed his arm. "Dad! Come on . . ."

He swung around in the seat and glared at me, his eyes blazing blue fire, and I thought he was going to hit me. He didn't, though. He just slammed the Ford into gear and burned out of there.

I mean, literally he laid a patch of rubber in the school parking lot. You could see it there the next day. A bunch of kids who were standing around smoking turned and stared admiringly as we peeled out onto the street. I guess my dad had become an instant hero with the local high school hoods, but I just felt embarrassed. And scared. Scared out of my mind, the way I always am when I know Dad's been drinking and he's driving. I know I don't seem like the nervous type, and I try hard not to let Dad see it, but in my mind I'm right back on that mountain highway, four years ago.

In some ways that night is clearer in my mind than yesterday, but I never have really straightened out whether Dad's drinking caused the accident or the accident caused the drinking. I guess they sort of caused each other.

It was late at night and raining. We were somewhere in Montana, and Dad was in a great mood. He was a top bull rider in those days, and he'd just won at another rodeo. That put him in third place and headed for the North American title again.

We were driving along with the windshield wipers swishing and "Me and Bobby McGee" playing on the radio. Dad loved that song, and he was singing along, flat, as usual. He had one arm around Mom, and I was kind of sandwiched in between, feeling warm and sleepy and secure. It's funny how clearly I remember that feeling. Maybe it's because that was the last time I've ever felt that way.

It was a winding road, climbing and twisting through the hills. We came around a sharp curve—maybe too fast —I don't know. Dad had been drinking a little. I didn't think he was drunk, but I guess at ten you're no expert.

Suddenly the whole road ahead was filled with blinding lights, and the huge shape of a logging truck, standing out a shade darker than the night sky.

I can't remember the crash, just the lights. And when I opened my eyes again, there were more lights, shining right in my face. I didn't know where I was, and I was scared to death. Then I saw this lady. She was dressed all in white, and she looked even shinier in all that bright light. I thought for a minute that I must be dead and she was an angel. But before I had time to decide if I was glad or sorry, she jabbed a big, long needle into my arm, and I knew she was no angel. Besides, she was fat and had a wart on her chin. I figured out that I must be in a hospital, and that scared me worse than being dead, so I started to holler for my mom and dad. The fat lady didn't pay any attention. Neither did any of the other white people who were standing around. That made me mad. Here I was, scared and hurt and bleeding, and these people wouldn't even let my parents in to see me. I was going to start hollering really loud, but then the one I'd decided must be the doctor said something that got my attention. "Hold him still now. I'm going to try to stitch that hand, and he isn't going to like it."

That should have made me completely hysterical, but for some reason it calmed me down instead. All I could think of was how proud my mom was going to be when she found out I didn't make a fuss. "Cowboys don't cry" was what she'd always say when I got banged up somehow. And since there was nothing in the world I wanted so much as to be a cowboy like my dad, you can bet I listened to her. She was always really proud of me when I didn't cry over little things.

It turned out that this wasn't a little thing. My right hand had gone through the windshield, and it was cut up so bad that I've still got the scar.

The doctor was right. I didn't like getting those stitches. It hurt worse than anything I've ever had, before or since, but I didn't cry. Not out loud, anyway. I just kept waiting for Mom to come and tell me how brave I was.

It seemed like that doctor was taking forever, but Mom still didn't come. Then, when he was almost finished with me, there was a knock on the door. I sighed with relief. I knew it was going to be Mom out there. She'd come in and put her arms around me, and everything would be okay.

A nurse opened the door. But it wasn't Mom who came in. It was Dad. He was sort of limping, and he had a big piece of tape above his eye, but outside of that he didn't seem to be hurt much. I sure was glad to see him.

"Dad!" I yelled. I would have run over and hugged him, but the nurse was still holding on to me.

"Hold on there, sonny. Just two or three more stitches."

By that time I'd just about forgot about being brave. "Dad, it hurts!" I half-sobbed. I think I would have had myself a good cry right then, but when Dad took a step forward, those bright, white lights caught his face, and I got a really good look at it. And what I saw scared the crying right out of me. Dad was as white as a ghost, and his eyes had a wild, shocked look. Something was wrong. Really wrong.

"Where's Mom? Dad, where is she? I want to see my mom!" I must have yelled it pretty loud because suddenly everything went dead quiet, and everybody in that emergency room was looking at us.

For a minute Dad just stood there, staring at me with that empty, helpless look on his face. Then finally he said in a voice that didn't even sound like him, "Your mom can't come, Shane."

"Why not?" I whispered, and I didn't sound like me, either.

Dad's voice didn't change. It was still flat and lifeless, but the words burned into me like he was shouting them at the top of his voice. " 'Cause she's dead."

The silence in that room hung like a heavy fog, and there, right in the middle of it, were Dad and I, staring at each other but not really even seeing each other. Maybe the fog was too thick.

Finally Dad seemed to sort of break loose. He took a step toward me and kind of held out his arms, and I thought, *He's gonna hold me. Dad's gonna put his arms around me and hold me, and somehow we're gonna make it 'cause we still got each other. . . .*

"Oh, Shane, I . . ." he started, and his voice sounded more real. I thought he was going to cry, but that was all right because if he cried, I could cry, too. But suddenly, halfway through that sentence and halfway through that step, he stopped and turned away. I heard him take a deep breath and swallow hard. "Shane, I got some things to take care of. I'll be back in a little while," he said in that empty voice again. He was almost running when he went out the door.

For some reason Mom's words came back then. And for the first time ever I wasn't sure I believed them. I figured maybe cowboys, even cowboys like my dad, needed to cry as much as anybody else. It was a long time later when I began to understand that maybe a guy like Dad couldn't cry. Maybe if he ever started, he'd never get stopped.

All I could think about right then was that I'd lost my mom, and it seemed like I was losing Dad, too. I couldn't figure out what I'd done to make him run away from me. When I got a little older, I realized it wasn't me he was running from, but that night I couldn't handle him leaving me that way any better than he could handle the fact that he'd driven into the accident that killed my mother.

The doctor went back to work on me then, and the fat nurse held me again, but somehow it was different, like she was really trying to keep it from hurting too much. But it didn't matter. When you get hurt bad enough, you don't feel any more pain. I didn't feel the rest of those stitches. I didn't feel much of anything for a while. All I knew was that I was waiting again. But this time I was waiting for my dad to come back to me.

Dad did come back, all right. But it seems like since that night I've never stopped waiting. Waiting for things that never happen. Waiting for Dad to get his life back together again. Waiting for him to make that one big ride that was going to start him on the way back to the top. Mostly, though, I've been waiting for him to stop trying to find the answers in the bottom of a bottle.

We kept following the rodeo circuit, more out of habit than anything. There wasn't really anywhere else to go. As long as I could remember, home for us had been wherever we unloaded the horses. And even if rodeoing isn't the easiest life, most of the time I liked it. At least while the rodeo was actually going on I could forget for a while and pretend that things were like they used to be.

I think it worked like that for Dad, too. Sometimes out there around the chutes when he was helping me get down on the steer I was going to ride, or I was handing him his bull rope, or we were both just hanging around with the other cowboys, Dad turned back into the guy he used to be . . . the guy I'd always wanted to grow up to be like. Watching him ride on those days, it wasn't hard to see what had made him North American Bull Riding Champion for the last two years. My dad had a lot of class, both in and out of the arena, and I was proud of him.

But, like I said, that was some days. Other days he'd get to drinking before the show and forget to turn up to ride at all. And instead of it getting better as time passed since the accident, it seemed like the good days started getting further and further apart. I couldn't have told you the exact time that it happened, but somewhere along the way I stopped being proud that he was my dad. I don't know if I stopped loving him. I couldn't tell. I knew I still loved the guy who used to be my dad, but it didn't seem like that guy was ever coming back.

Finally, about two years ago, things hit an all-time low. Dad was riding so bad that he was hardly ever making any money. If something didn't change soon, we were going to starve. Then, one day, the rodeo clown didn't turn up at one show. I guess the rodeo contractor was pretty desperate, and he must have known Dad was getting desperate, too.

"Morgan," he said, "grab yourself some baggy pants, paint your nose a little redder than it already is, and get out there and keep those bulls from trampling the cowboys for half an hour, and you've got yourself a hundred bucks."

Dad jumped at the chance, and I was glad. My personal opinion was that he wasn't anything but a clown anymore, so he might as well be getting paid for it.

Anyway, he turned out to be a good clown. In spite of being a drunk, Dad probably knew as much about bulls as anybody in the rodeo business, and he'd been a rider long enough to know that lives depend on the clown. So he stayed sober while he was working. Finally that job became permanent. That's why it says *Josh Morgan—Rodeo Clown* on our old Ford truck.

After Dad got the job, there was a little more money, enough for meals, clothes, and gas. But things still weren't going too great. We both knew we didn't have a future. Someday Dad was going to wake up still without a cent to his name and too old to be a bull clown. And I was going to find myself grown up without ever having stayed in one place long enough to get a proper education or even make a real friend.

But Dad has never been the kind of guy to think about tomorrow, and I wasn't in any position to do it for him, so we just kept drifting, waiting for the big break to come along.

Then, surprisingly enough, the break came. My dad got a letter from a lawyer. That scared both of us, at first. Anything we'd had to do with lawyers had been the result of the accident, and all of the news had been bad.

I guess this was bad news, too, in a way. My mom's father had just died. I might have felt bad about it if I'd ever had a chance to get to know him. But, for one thing, he lived away up in Alberta somewhere, and we were in the States all the time except for when we hit the Calgary Stampede every July.

The other thing was that Grandpa White and Dad had no use for each other. Grandpa had practically disowned Mom when she married Dad, but we did visit Grandpa once, when I was about five years old. That was a long time ago, and about all I remember is the fight. Well, maybe not a fight. They never did hit each other, but they came close. And would you believe it all started because Grandpa told Dad he didn't like the way he parked his truck? Dad didn't like anybody telling him anything, and the next thing I knew, he was calling Grandpa a fat-headed farmer. Grandpa called him an irresponsible Irish idiot.

I can see now that it was a fairly accurate description of my father, but in those days I was young enough to think that Dad could do no wrong. I picked up a handful of rocks and started chucking them at Grandpa. Then Mom got so mad at all three of us that she started crying. And my mom was not the crying type.

It turned out to be a short visit. We hadn't been back since.

Now Grandpa was dead, and the letter was to tell us that we had inherited his land. Maybe that sounds simple enough. It wasn't.

First of all, the only reason he let Dad anywhere near the place was because, since my grandmother had been dead for years and Mom was their only child, I was the only close relative he had left. And, like it or not, until I was eighteen, Dad was in charge of me.

But, even dead, my grandfather didn't give up without a fight. After a few *therefore*'s and *whereas*'es the letter got

down to the nitty-gritty, which sounded like Grandpa
had dictated it word-for-word to the lawyer.

"Since my daughter is dead, my property should right-
fully go to her son, Shane Morgan. But he being under-
age, against my better judgment, I am leaving it to Josh
Morgan to hold in trust until my grandson reaches the
age of eighteen.

"Furthermore, I stipulate that before receiving title to
this property Josh Morgan will provide proof that he and
the boy have taken up permanent residence there."

It took a while to absorb all that, but finally two things
stuck out in my mind. One: We had a quarter section of
land. And two: Taking up permanent residence meant
no more following the rodeo circuit. Dad might have
outlived Grandpa, but Grandpa had still managed to get
in the last word. He had just grounded Dad as effectively
as if he had been a naughty kid who'd stayed out too late.

At first, hearing the whole thing about inheriting the
land, I couldn't believe I was wide-awake. Having a place
to go home to had been a dream for so long. But, hard as
I tried, I never could tell how Dad really felt about the
whole thing. I knew that he and Mom had always used to
talk about how someday they were going to get a ranch of
their own, and there sure didn't seem to be any other way
that Dad would ever get enough money together to buy a
place. But things were a lot different now with Mom
gone. I had a feeling that if it hadn't been for me, Dad
might have just said "No, thank you" to that lawyer and
kept on going down the road.

He didn't do that. He hunted up the lawyer as soon as
he could, and we signed the papers together. I'll always
remember him laying down the pen afterward and saying, "Well, there it is, kid. You got yourself a ranch." He

sort of paused and then added, "And a future." He was grinning at me, but there was still something sad about the way he said it. But the part that I've never been able to forget is that he didn't say "we," just "you." It made me feel guilty somehow. Like he was giving up a whole way of life for me. Sometimes I wondered if maybe always moving was the only way he had of staying ahead of a lot of bad memories that kept following him. What would happen when he settled down in one place long enough for them to catch up to him? I didn't try to find an answer to that one. Just the question scared me bad enough.

2

I came back to the present with a jerk as Dad swerved to miss a pothole and drove smack into a bigger one. Deer Valley might be a nice enough town, but its streets could use some work.

Then we were across the river and heading out into the country. Suddenly it struck me. We were going to our own place.

Yesterday, when we came over that hill and I got my first glimpse of that little white house with a grove of big, old spruce trees standing guard around it, I got the weirdest feeling that I'd lived there all my life; I felt as if I belonged there just like those trees did, and the creek, and the bunch of white-tailed deer that went bounce-jumping off across the field.

I suppose to most people it would have just looked like a run-down old farm with a lot of fallen-down fences and a barn that needed painting. To me it looked like home. The thought of getting back there again made me feel so good I almost forgot to be nervous about Dad's driving.

Anyway, he seemed to be sobering up some, and his

temper had cooled down enough so that he was only driving on one side of the road at a time. That's one thing about Dad. No matter how mad he gets, he always gets over it fast. I'm just the opposite. It takes a lot to get me really mad, but I can hold a grudge for a long time.

Right now, though, I was getting in a good enough mood even to forgive Dad for making me an instant celebrity at Deer Valley School. I turned down the radio and asked, "Well, did you get finished moving in?"

He gave me that half-funny, half-serious look of his and said, "Sure did. It was a big job, but I got it done. I put your clothes in one bedroom and mine in the other and the saddles in the barn and . . ." He paused. "And then we were all moved in."

We both started to laugh. It was sure a good thing that all of Grandpa's stuff was still in the house. We were going to need it.

Seeing Dad laugh like that reminded me of the way things used to be, when there was more to laugh about. *Maybe*, I thought, *maybe if we settle down here, he'll change. Maybe we can be like a family again and* . . . I stopped myself fast. When you start counting on what might be, you start getting hurt. It had taken me long enough to learn that, and I didn't plan to forget it for a while. If things were good, I'd make the most of it, but I wasn't expecting any guarantees.

We were a few miles out of town now, and heading west. The mountains must have been at least fifty miles away, but the air was so clear they looked close enough to touch. And, after spending so long in dry country, I could hardly believe that any place could be as green as Alberta in the spring. Suddenly I wanted to get home fast and start exploring our place. I almost wished Dad would drive a little faster . . . almost.

But he was starting to relax and get in a visiting mood. He looked over at me and asked, "So how'd they treat you at school? Sure hope they ain't all as ornery as that fat principal."

I wasn't going to touch that one, so I just shrugged and said, "Okay, I guess." Actually I hadn't been there long enough to find out much about the place. We'd slept in this morning, and Dad had dropped me off there at noon. I'd had to fill out a bunch of registration papers, and then they gave me something called a placement test. I had gone to school regularly enough to know I was supposed to be in grade eight, but this test was supposed to put me in the right group.

Well, I don't know what happened, but after the guidance counselor checked the test, he looked me over real careful like he couldn't figure out what had happened either. "Well, Shane, you did very well. Especially on the reading section." He gave me that puzzled look again and I knew he was having trouble making the connection between the scruffy kid in the faded jeans and the high scores he was reading from my test. "You must do a bit of reading on your own, eh, Shane?" he asked, after looking the test over one more time.

I couldn't help smiling to myself at that one. It was probably the understatement of the year. I guess you could almost class me as a bookaholic. I'm hooked on books about as bad as Dad is hooked on booze, and for the same reasons. I've always liked reading and, since Mom always had her nose in a book, I picked up the habit pretty young. But it wasn't till after Mom was gone that I really got into reading so much. I can still remember the night that I never went to sleep at all, just kept on read-ing.

It was somewhere in Oregon. Dad had left me in a hotel room and said he was going out for a little while. Only he ended up getting in a fight in the bar and getting jailed overnight. I couldn't go to sleep. I kept wondering where he was and if he was ever coming back, so, for something to do, I picked up one of the Louis L'Amour westerns Dad always buys, and started reading. And sud-denly I found out something special about books. They're a place to escape to when you can't really go anywhere. As long as I kept reading, I could just make myself disappear into the story and not be scared or worried or lonesome, nothing—I didn't even have to be myself anymore.

By the time Dad staggered in the next morning, I was almost finished the third book. I've been reading every-thing I can lay my hands on ever since.

I looked up at the counsellor. "Yeah, I read some," I said.

He nodded. "I thought so," he said and then added, "According to these results you'll be in the Advanced Group. Let's go and meet your new class."

I just sort of gulped. Advanced Group? Did this guy have any idea how much school I'd missed in the past few years? I didn't think any amount of reading would make up for that. Test or no test, I wasn't sure I was going to fit into any Advanced Group.

When I got a look at the kids there, I was sure I wouldn't. I don't mean there was anything wrong with them. They mostly wore blue jeans and T-shirts and running shoes, and I noticed that one or two even had on riding boots, but there was just something about them that spelled "class." Like their blue jeans were hand-faded or something. I was already sure they were smarter than I was, and I added the fact that they sure looked a lot richer, too. The combination left me with the feeling that I came from the wrong side of the tracks—which isn't easy since Deer Valley doesn't have a railroad.

I didn't tell Dad any of that, though. He'd just get steamed up again, and I didn't want that to happen. Right now he was looking as self-satisfied as a cat with a mouse in its mouth. Obviously he knew something I didn't know. I tried for some information. "So what else did you do this afternoon?"

"Didn't have time for much more. Had company."

"Company? But you don't know any—" I stopped right there because at that moment we topped a little hill, and our yard lay spread out below. The first thing I saw was the brown truck hitched to a four-horse trailer.

"Jeff's here!" I yelled. "Did he bring the horses?"

Dad laughed. "What do you think? He hauled that rig all the way up from Cheyenne just to see if the wheels went around?"

I didn't have time to think up a smart answer because the second the truck stopped, I was out and running across the yard.

There they were in the corral, all four of them. The way I went tearing over there and then jumped off the top rail it's funny I didn't spook them into the next county. But they were kind of tired from the trip. Besides, they're used to me. We've been friends for a long time.

They were looking good. Jeff Burdette always takes good care of his horses, which was the only reason I could stand it when we had to sell our trailer and leave

ours at his place. Besides being a stock contractor and
calf roper, Jeff runs a roping school, and he said he could
always use extra horses so he'd keep ours for the use of
them once in a while. I always kind of suspected that he
didn't use them much but was just saying that so Dad's
pride didn't get hurt. Dad and Jeff go back a long ways.
In fact, Dad helped Jeff get his start in rodeo. Then it
seemed that about the time Dad's luck all went bad, Jeff's
went good. He's a big name around rodeo now, but he's
still Dad's buddy.

The horses started crowding around me, pushing and
jostling one another to get closer. They seemed as glad
to see me as I was to see them. But I knew all this affection wasn't without a motive. Oats. Horses are awful oat
addicts, and my horse, Reb, is one of the worst. I think
he'd mug an old lady if she had some rolled oats in her
grocery bag, and right now he was sure I must be hiding
some somewhere. He just about ate me up before I finally convinced him that the oats would come later and
he settled for a scratch behind the ear. As he leaned his
chin on my shoulder and nuzzled my shirt I wondered
how I'd got along without him for nearly a year. He's a
great old horse, not purebred or anything. His sire was a
Thoroughbred, and his mother was part Welsh pony, but
Reb turned out looking more like a Morgan than anything else.

He used to be a barrel horse, and he was pretty fast,
too. The only problem was that he had a sense of humor.
Every once in a while he'd decide not to bother with the
third barrel. He'd just take the bit in his teeth (and he's
one of the hardest-mouthed horses I've ever seen) and
head right out of the arena after the second barrel. And
since nobody has ever picked up prize money on a horse

that didn't finish running the cloverleaf pattern and doing the turns around all three barrels, the girl who owned
him didn't think it was funny.

She tried everything to break him of that, but it was no
use. She was crazy over that horse and hated to give him
up, but Mom finally convinced her that he'd have a good
home, so she sold him to us.

Shawnee is a big, heavy-muscled buckskin. She's Dad's
horse, but I can ride her as long as I don't "go racin' her
or givin' her any fool notions," which about covers anything that might be fun, so I don't usually bother with
her.

The old sorrel mare is Goldie. She's pushing twenty
and mainly retired. But in her day she's done it all. Dad
roped with her, and Mom barrel raced, and even flat-
raced her at rodeos. She's not a very big horse, but she
used to be one of the fastest short-distance runners
around. She's also Angel's mother.

Angel. She's four years old. A dark palomino with a
white mane and tail and a blaze face. Her sire was a top
racing-type quarter horse, and she's about the most
beautiful animal I've ever seen. It really tears me up that
I can't ride her. Nobody can because she's not broke.
Sometimes I doubt that she ever will be.

Angel was Mom's horse. Dad gave her to Mom on the
day she was foaled, and I'd never seen Mom so proud of
anything. I can remember her laughing, but still half-
serious, saying, "All right, you guys. This little angel is
my horse, and I'm going to train her personally, so just
keep your hands off her." She had Angel halter-broke
before the accident, but nobody's done anything with
her since.

I was standing there watching the sun catch the golden

ripple of her muscles and wondering if I could ever get up the nerve to ask Dad to let me break her when suddenly a big hand came down hard on my shoulder. I just about jumped the fence before I came back to reality and heard a deep voice drawl, "Hey, Short Stuff! Ain't you even comin' in the house to eat?"

It was the same old Jeff Burdette. He stood six-foot-four and was built like a grizzly bear, but he acted more like an overgrown Saint Bernard pup.

He pushed the black Stetson that was his trademark back far enough for me to see that he really did have eyes and looked me over like a horse he was considering buying. "You know, kid," he said at last, "I do believe there is some hope you ain't gonna be a midget all your life after all. Now, if only your brain would start growin' . . ."

I took a swing at him like I always do when he comes out with his crackpot comments. And, just like he always does, he ducked, grabbed me in a bear hug, and held me dangling about two feet off the ground.

"Someday," I gasped as I turned red from lack of air, "I'm gonna get bigger than you, and I'm gonna take you down and sit on you, and squash you flatter than an ant under an elephant!"

He set me down just in time to avoid the need for artificial respiration and said, "Well, if you've got such big plans, you'd better get in the house and get some of my red-hot Mexican chili under your belt to start you growin'."

"You, uh, made your Mexican chili?" I said faintly. I had eaten Jeff's chili before.

"You bet! Wait'll you taste it."

"Looks like somebody already did."

"Huh?"

"He didn't make it," I said, pointing to a bleached buffalo skull someone had hung on the barn wall.

Jeff may be tougher than I am, but I'm faster than he is. I was sitting at the table, looking innocent, by the time he caught up to me.

I knew I had to be up in time to catch the school bus in the morning, so I went to bed fairly early and left Dad and Jeff swapping lies about the good old days. I'd heard most of the stories a hundred times anyway, and most of the time they just made me sad because I knew those days weren't ever coming back, no matter how much they were talked about.

The chili had definitely been the super-hot Mexican kind. I had to get up three times for a drink of water, which, in turn, caused me to get up two more times. Every time I got up, the light was still on in the kitchen, and Jeff and Dad were still reliving every rodeo they ever rode in.

Talking usually made Dad thirsty, and with the chili for an added excuse I didn't figure he'd be feeling too swift in the morning. If I planned to be up in time to catch the bus, I'd have to take matters into my own hands. I dug out my old alarm clock and set it for six-thirty. Then I lay awake thinking of how I hated being scared out of a sound sleep by the sound of the alarm. Finally I decided that if I stuffed it under my pillow, the vibration would probably wake me, but I wouldn't have to hear that awful noise. At last I went to sleep.

The clock woke me up, all right, but not in the way I had planned. I turned over in my sleep and dragged the pillow with me. The clock rolled out onto the floor. The crash left me wide awake, blinking in the gray light of dawn at the carcass of the clock, lying there with its quivering insides spilling across the floor.

I groaned and stuffed the whole mess in a drawer. For some reason I suddenly remembered the words I'd seen on a poster once. "Today is the first day of the rest of your life."

Wow.

3

My prediction was right. Dad and Jeff were definitely not bright-eyed and bushy-tailed the next morning. I thought about making them breakfast just to get even with Jeff for the chili, but I'm not that sadistic.

I checked the fridge to find myself something to eat. The choices were limited. Half a pint of licorice ice cream —well, you can't eat that for breakfast. The only other thing I could find was the rest of the chili.

Licorice ice cream wasn't such a bad breakfast, after all.

I walked out to the road early and watched the morning spread over our valley. Ribbons of fog floated above the creek and the other low places, giving it a haunted look, making a perfect setting for a movie called something like *The Thing from Fog Valley*. But the sun was touching the tips of the spruce trees on the hills to the west, lighting them like candles. In a few minutes sunshine would pour through the whole valley and "The Thing" would be gone forever. I might have had the whole screenplay written in my mind if the bus hadn't come just then.

I climbed up the steps, and the driver pointed to the only empty seat, which happened to be the one right behind the door. Bad news. First, because, as any kid who's ever ridden a school bus knows, at the back is where the action is. Any kid over ten who hasn't at least graduated to the back half of the bus is a dead loss.

Second, in the front seat, everybody can see you, and you can't see anybody unless you turn around and stare. I wanted to do that because I had caught a glimpse of a blond girl who rated a second look. Her hair was the same color as Angel's mane, and her conformation didn't look bad either. But everybody was already studying me like a bug under a microscope, so I didn't look back.

I looked beside me instead and discovered a six-year-old ankle-biter who looked like he could use a Kleenex. I didn't know too much about little kids except that they usually talked too much and seemed to throw up quite often in moving vehicles.

I sighed. I should have known that the alarm clock incident was a bad omen for the day and gone back to bed. But school didn't start too badly, considering. When I discovered that the blonde from the bus was in my class, things began to look a lot better.

The teachers really threw the work at you in that hot-shot class, but I didn't have too much trouble. After all, if you can read and write, you can do language arts, and science and social studies are mainly common sense.

Then we got to math. And I found out that there was a whole pile of stuff that I'd never heard of. I was pretty good at multiplying and dividing and decimals and fractions and stuff like that, but when the teacher started talking about things like the intersection of sets, it could have been the road report for all I knew. And for all I cared. But I kept that part to myself because I've never found a school yet where they were particularly interested in hearing that type of opinion. The teacher gave me eight pages of homework to help me catch up. Help like that could do permanent emotional damage.

At long last it was noon, and I was dying for some fresh air. I've never figured out why they always heat schools as if they're trying to grow tropical plants in them.

There was a football game going, and I recognized some guys from my class playing. I thought about seeing if I could get in the game, but then I decided I wasn't in the mood to get knocked down and trampled on just then.

I thought I'd just walk around and get the feel of the place, instead. I wandered into the parking lot, and there was the same bunch of guys I'd seen there yesterday afternoon. They were leaning on a car, smoking again.

I took a good look at them and knew that my first impression had been right. They were not my kind of people. I'll admit I probably come on as being a fairly tough kid—you don't survive my kind of life-style by being a boy scout. But these guys were ridiculous. They looked like a cross between redneck hillbillies and punk rockers. I did not want to get acquainted. I walked a little faster and tried pretending they didn't exist.

A voice caught up to me. "Hey, kid. Wanna smoke?"

I stopped walking. "No, thanks. I don't smoke." It was the truth. I'd tried it a few times, and Dad wouldn't have stopped me, but it just never did that much for me. A lot of cowboys smoke, but it's no big macho symbol for them, in spite of what the Marlboro Man may think. The truth is that every rodeo kid's idea of being supercool is a can of Copenhagen. You carry it in your back pocket until it wears a circle into your jeans. Then you're "in." It doesn't much matter if you ever chew the stuff, just as long as the can's in your pocket. I've had the same can for about a year, and I've chewed a little, but it's fairly gross stuff, especially if you get confused and swallow. Anyway, it reminds me too much of the brown goop you get on your hand if you pick up a grasshopper.

I started walking again, but I knew it wasn't going to work. I'd been the new kid in enough schools to know what the routine was like.

"He don't smoke!" one of the bunch squeaked in a high voice.

Another one spoke up. "Well, the kid sure ain't as tough as his old man, is he?"

"Who's his old man?"

"Aw, you remember, Rob. The one that parks in the bus lane."

"You mean the drunk that was mouthin' off to old Petersen?"

"That's him. The clown. The real, honest-to-goodness, walkin'-around, fallin'-down-drunk clown."

I took a deep breath. *He's right,* I thought. *What he's saying is what I've said to myself a hundred times. But for some reason that I don't even come close to understanding, I'm going to get myself into a whole pile of trouble because I can't stand hearing this jerk say it.*

At that moment I couldn't have said who I hated worse, the kid for saying it, or Dad for making it the truth.

I turned around slowly and looked the guy over. He

was big. And he didn't look like a real intellectual type, either. In fact, I wouldn't have been surprised if his IQ and his shirt size were dangerously close to intersecting. (Math, remember?)

When scared out of your wits, attack. That was a piece of advice Jeff had handed out once. I had wondered at the time who a guy Jeff's size could find to be scared of, but I knew I was scared now. I glanced around for a teacher, but they're just like cops, never around when you need one. Except for a bunch of girls standing over by the school, and us, the parking lot was empty.

I walked up to the big guy and gave him a cold glare. "You'd better shut your mouth, punk."

He laughed. "You plannin' to make me?"

"If I have to."

Then he said it. That familiar four-letter friend-getter, and on top of everything else he'd said, it was more than I could take right then. I took a swing at him and felt a satisfying jolt as I connected with his big nose, which started to bleed all over his Heavy Metal T-shirt. He didn't even stagger, just looked surprised. Then he charged. He reminded me of a big Brahma I'd once seen go right through an arena fence and into the grandstand. He wasn't hard to dodge at first, and I even got in a couple more good punches, but then his buddies kind of closed in, and there wasn't much room to move. One of his wild punches connected with a couple of ribs I'd busted riding steers last fall, and it hurt so bad that for a second I thought he'd stabbed me. I doubled over . . . and met his other fist with my chin. My legs went rubbery, and as the pavement came up to meet me I remembered that I'd passed up football because I didn't want to get knocked down and trampled.

But I didn't have much time to regret that move because this gorilla turned out to be a real street fighter. He used his boots, too. I rolled just in time to miss getting kicked to kingdom come, but I knew that was inevitable if I didn't get up. So I did . . . right into a punch in the eye. I was beginning to think I was going to die, and I was just hoping it wouldn't take too long.

"Knock it off, Bart!" The voice was loud enough to penetrate the cobwebs that were starting to close in around my mind. My first thought was that if it was my head they wanted knocked off, old Bart wasn't doing a bad job.

But whoever was yelling at him sure got Bart's attention. He stopped dead and stood there gawking. Then I saw the reason. It was the girl, the blonde. I hadn't even found out her name yet, but she already seemed to have become an important part of my life.

I couldn't believe the way she had just walked up and started yelling at the toughest guy around. "What are you trying to do? Kill him? Quit trying to prove what a big man you are! Just get out of here and leave him alone!"

Bart didn't say anything. He wasn't getting the chance. I hoped he wasn't in the habit of hitting girls, but if he was, I would have bet that here was one girl who would have hit him back. She was some steamed up.

But all Bart did was glare at her. Then suddenly he swore under his breath and turned and stalked away. His friends melted into the crowd that had gathered.

Then the girl turned that level gray gaze on me, and I understood why Bart couldn't think of anything to say.

"Are you okay?" she asked quietly.

Well, what are you supposed to say when a girl rescues

you? "Yeah, sure," I said, too fast. I didn't know if I was okay or a terminal case. But even with my shirt torn, my lip bleeding, and my eye swelling shut, there was no way my pride would let me say anything else. Not to her, anyway.

The bell rang then, and the crowd started moving away. I wondered how good the chances were of making it into the washroom and getting cleaned up before I ran into any teachers.

The chances weren't good. Suddenly I found myself face-to-face with a big man. He was wearing a purple necktie, and it really was ugly.

"I think you'd better come into my office," he growled.

The girl was still standing there, watching us walk away.

4

"All right, Shane, I think you'd better give it to me straight." The principal wasn't exactly smiling.

I shrugged. "There's nothing to tell. We just got into a fight."

He gave me a hard look. "There are four hundred kids who use this school yard every day. The other three hundred and ninety-eight did not just get into a fight. There is no such thing as just getting into a fight. There had to be a reason."

He paused, and I think I was supposed to say something, but I couldn't think of anything he'd want to hear.

"Who started it?" he shot at me suddenly.

"It depends on what you call starting it." I wasn't trying to be mouthy, but it seemed like things were beginning to come out that way.

Mr. Petersen stood up. "Let's get something straight right now. I called you in here to hear what you had to say for yourself first because I don't know anything about you, and I do know something about the way Bart Willard operates. But I don't plan to sit here playing games with you. Now, who started the fight?"

I thought it over for a while. Then I looked the principal in the eye and said, "I threw the first punch, if that's what you mean."

"Why did you hit him?"

I thought that one over for longer. This guy really believed I was going to give him all the gory details. Well, it doesn't work that way. There are some things you just don't tell teachers. And one of those things is that your father's a drunk but you can't let a guy like Bart Willard get away with saying so.

The silence got long and heavy.

The principal sighed. "Okay, have it your way." Then his voice turned steely. "But if you think you can come into a new school and start throwing your weight around on your first day, you've got it all wrong. I'm going to have my eye on you from now on, and if you do anything —anything to make me notice you . . ." He broke off there and took a really good look at me. "Anyway, whatever you did to start this business, you don't look like you need any further punishment. You might as well go home for the rest of the day. What's your phone number? I'll have your mother come and pick you up."

"My mother's dead." My voice had a strange, flat sound. Even after all these years those words don't get any easier to say.

Mr. Petersen looked embarrassed. "I'm sorry, Shane. You live with your father, then . . ." Suddenly he got a funny look on his face, like a light bulb had just flashed on, and I knew he'd just made the connection between me and the crazy cowboy who had parked in the bus lane.

"What's his number?" he repeated. I didn't say anything. I was already imagining a second meeting between him and Dad. Compared to that, a rematch with Bart Willard would have been a real pleasure.

"Come on, Shane. Do I have to look it up in the school records?"

"Eight three six, five four two two," I said tiredly.

He dialed and waited through about eight rings before he hung up. "That's too bad. He isn't home," he said.

Thank God, I added silently.

"How are you feeling?"

I was feeling like I'd been run over by a buffalo stampede. "Okay, I guess," I said.

"All right, then. Get cleaned up as well as you can and go back to class."

I walked out of the office and stopped at the fountain outside for a drink. I went on into the washroom and took a look at my face in the mirror. It looked like bomb damage, but a little soap and water improved things a lot. The eye was black, all right, though I'd had worse ones, and the cut lip was swelled a little. Outside of that, I didn't look too bad. Then I noticed that there was a little cut at the corner of my eyebrow, and it had bled all over my hair on that side. Ordinarily my hair is just streaky dark blond, but this patch had turned a real neat strawberry blond color. I kind of hated to wash it out.

My shirt was a write-off. Clothes don't get repaired much around our place at the best of times, but I don't think plastic surgery would have saved this one. I threw it in the garbage can and put on my faded denim jacket.

I started slowly down the hall toward homeroom, hating the thought of walking in in front of everybody. I knocked on the door as quietly as I could, and Miss Bradley, our language teacher, opened it. She stared at me for a minute and then asked, "Are you okay?" so softly that no one in the class even looked up. I nodded. "All right then, we're working on spelling, page forty-two. Just sit down and get started."

I gave her a grateful but crooked smile and sat down.

The afternoon wasn't half bad. I could tell that the other kids were all dying of curiosity about what had happened, but they had enough class not to let it show too much. Mainly they were just extra friendly, and during our free period I had so much help that I got about half the eight pages of math done.

I had a feeling that anybody who tangled with Bart Willard automatically made a lot of friends. And at least one bad enemy.

But I wasn't worrying about that right now. I was too busy trying to figure out how I felt about the blond girl. She seemed to be kind of avoiding me in class, and I was glad, because every time I thought about her, I got confused. I mean, being rescued by a girl . . .

The final bell rang, and I ran for the bus, thinking about how good it would be to get home and talk to someone quiet and sensible—like Reb.

The little kid in the seat beside me took one look at me and then just sat there with his mouth open. Finally he had his wits gathered enough to say, "You've got a black eye." At least the kid wasn't stone-blind.

After another minute of serious thinking he asked, "What happened to your eye?"

"Oh, I just walked into a doorknob," I said, wishing he'd shut up.

"It must have been a pretty high doorknob."

"Yeah."

"You'd better be more careful. You could get really hurt if you don't watch where you're going."

He should have told me that before I tried going across the parking lot.

5

Our truck was in the yard, but Jeff's wasn't. The house had a been-empty-all-day feeling about it. It was my second day with a place to call home, but I was already learning that home isn't so great unless there's someone to come home to.

I wandered around the house aimlessly until I noticed a piece of paper torn from a grocery bag lying on the table. I picked it up and read:

> Shane—Jeff and I went to Cochrane to look at a horse he might buy. Don't worry if we're late and don't forget to feed the horses.
>
> Dad

I read it through twice. Something about it bothered me. Cochrane—I'd seen that name somewhere not long ago. But where? Then I remembered I'd been reading a *Calgary Sun* last night. (It was actually the Sunshine Girl I remembered.) The paper was still lying on a chair. I started flipping through it.

There it was, in big, black letters. COCHRANE RO-

DEO MAY 30. And I didn't need to check the calendar to know that was today. I threw the paper across the room. To see a horse! Who did Dad think he was kidding? If he was going rodeoing, why didn't he just say so? I couldn't have stopped him.

When I was little, he always gave me a licking if I lied to him. So what was I supposed to do to him when he lied to me?

That question was still replaying in my mind like a stuck record as I ran outside and saddled up Reb. He was tired of standing around in that corral, and I could tell that if Jeff had used him at all, it had been a long time ago. From the looks of him Reb had spent most of his time out in the pasture, eating grass and getting fat.

As soon as I hit the saddle, he ducked his head and lit into crow-hopping across the pasture. I should have pulled up his head and yelled at him, but I was in a mood to enjoy it. It didn't take long for him to work the kinks out of his backbone and settle down to a gallop, but he was still fighting the bit, wanting to run. Well, that was fine with me. I had a few things I wanted to leave behind.

"Okay, baby, you wanna run? Run!" I dug my heels into his ribs, and he flattened out into a dead run. The narrow, overgrown trail led uphill, through the woods. Trees on both sides flashed past in a blur, and low branches reached out to grab at me as Reb sailed over fallen logs without even breaking stride. Springy poplar branches slashed at my face like whips, but I didn't care. Every time Reb slowed down a little, I touched him with my heels, and he leaped ahead like I'd hit him. Reb's like that. He'll run himself to death before he'll quit on you.

We must have gone about half a mile before I started thinking straight again. I touched Reb's neck with my hand and realized it was soaking wet. Streaks of white lather stood out where the reins had rubbed his neck. I could feel his sides heaving under my legs.

What did I think I was doing, taking a soft horse that hadn't worked for months and running him that fast, that far? You could kill a horse that way.

Real classy, Shane, I thought as I reined him in. *Life kicks you around a little, so you take it out on a horse that can't fight back.*

I jumped off and loosened the cinch so Reb could breathe a little easier, then stood there, stroking his sweaty nose and hating myself. "Sorry, baby, I didn't mean to do that to you." He gave me a kind of forgiving look and rubbed his wet, itchy head on me so hard he almost knocked me over.

By the time he was done, my jacket looked and smelled like I'd used it to give him a rubdown. It had been a bad day for clothes . . . among other things.

I turned toward home, leading Reb. He'd need the walk to cool off. Just as I turned I caught a glimpse of glass, shining in the late-afternoon sun.

Through the trees I could see the fence that marked our west boundary, and beyond that a couple of hundred yards was a layout so fancy I thought I must have accidently tuned in to *Dallas.*

The house was big enough to pass for a hotel, with porches and patios and so many decks it should have carried lifeboats. And beyond the house were dozens of stables and sheds, all surrounded by miles of white-painted plank fence.

"Wow! Get a load of the neighbors, Reb!"

Reb wasn't impressed. He snorted, blowing his nose all over me, and shook his head, impatient to get going.

"You don't appreciate class when you see it, you little scrub," I told him and scratched behind his ears for him.

I was feeling a little better about life in general by the time I'd walked him home. I was also feeling hungry, so I gave him a quick rubdown and put him in the corral with the other horses. Then I went to the barn for hay. There were six bales left. Three days' feed. And then what? Buy some more? I didn't know what Dad was planning to use for money. Dad hadn't worked any rodeos for a month, and clowns sure don't get holiday pay.

Feeding hay didn't make sense anyway. There was grass six inches high everywhere, and the land was fenced. The horses would be better off out grazing.

I opened the gate and stepped back. They eyed me suspiciously, wondering if this was a trick and trying to decide whether they could make a break for it before I could slam the gate in their faces.

Angel finally made the first move. Daintily, like she was walking on eggs, she trotted up to the gateway and stopped, watching me out of the corner of her eye. Then she lowered her head and snorted at the ground, blowing up little puffs of dust.

She made up her mind and stepped outside, then hesitated a couple of seconds. Suddenly she ducked her head, kicked up her heels, and tore out of there, bucking and snorting like an outlaw bronc, and flying her blond tail like a banner. The others were on her heels, and I stood and watched them all disappear like kids on the last day of school.

Well, I'd solved that problem, I thought as I turned toward the empty house. Now, like it or not, if I wasn't planning to starve to death, I was going to have to do some cooking.

I checked the fridge and wasn't too surprised to find the chili still there. I wondered if I was desperate enough to eat it. Not quite. I checked a cupboard. Canned vegetables. I wasn't that desperate either. Another cupboard and . . . jackpot! About a dozen packages of Kraft Dinner. Suddenly I was sure that Grandpa White and I did share some common genes . . . if genes are what determine that the only thing you know how to cook is Kraft Dinner.

I found a great big pot in the cupboard and got the macaroni boiling. I wouldn't have minded a glass of milk, but there wasn't any, so I settled for warming up the breakfast coffee. It was about thick enough to be crunchy, but I'm not fussy.

It was beginning to sound awful quiet in the house, so I hauled the pot of macaroni and my coffee into the living room, pulled the drapes, and turned on the TV. This place had two channels. Two! Even the worst hick towns in Montana usually had five. And these two were both having news.

Well, the social studies teacher seemed real hung up on current events, so I watched. There was a bunch of political stuff which just about put me to sleep. Then they shifted to some on-location shots of one of those Middle East places . . . Lebanon, I think. There were all these little kids standing around in what was left of their bombed-out houses, looking so scared and lost. Others were dead, lying in little heaps like old, thrown-away dolls that no one wanted anymore. I got mad just thinking about how people could do things like that. I didn't understand it at all. But it made me do some thinking about my own problems. My life-style might not ever win the *Good Housekeeping* Seal of Approval, but I sure wasn't ready to trade places.

I was still thinking that over when the seven o'clock movie came on, and it made me start feeling sorry for myself again. It was an old Jimmy Stewart film called *Shenandoah*. I thought it was going to be a western, but it turned out to be a Civil War movie, which was just as good.

I really got hooked on that movie. Jimmy Stewart played the father of this whole family of nearly grown-up kids. His wife was dead, and he missed her a lot, but that just seemed to make him care even more about his kids. He was really a neat guy. I wished things like that happened in real life, especially my real life.

The film was almost over when things started getting really tense. Old Jimmy and his whole family were riding straight into an ambush when . . . there was a loud knock on the door. I went straight up, as if somebody'd shot me.

A few minutes later I was wishing somebody had.

When I opened the door, two things surprised me. First, it was still daylight outside. I'd lost all track of time, and it could have been midnight for all I knew.

And second, I was looking at the last person I had expected to see again today.

6

Standing there in a pair of patched jeans and an old jacket that looked as dirty as mine, and with her long blond hair hanging in windblown tangles, the girl looked great. But she also looked upset.

"Hi" was all I could think of to say, especially since I still hadn't found out her name.

"Shane," she said, out of breath like she'd run a long way, "you've got horses in the pasture along the road?"

"Yeah," I said slowly, wondering what it was to her and getting the feeling that I didn't want to hear whatever was coming next.

"One of them's hung up in an old barbed wire fence there, and she's really tearing herself up."

I felt the bottom drop out of my stomach. "Which horse?" I asked, so low I could barely hear it myself.

"The palomino."

Oh, God, no! Please, not Angel.

I was already on my way out the door.

"Isn't your dad here? We're gonna need help to get her out of there."

"My dad's never around when I need him!" I yelled over my shoulder. I hadn't meant to say that, but sometimes when you're upset enough, you accidentally tell the truth.

I dragged the toolbox out of the truck and started pawing through it, looking for the wire cutter.

"We'll need a halter," she said.

"In the barn."

She was back with it by the time I had found the cutter.

"It's quite a ways. We can ride double." For the first time I noticed the blue roan horse standing ground-tied in the yard.

She got on and took her foot out of the stirrup so I could get up behind her. I don't think that horse had ever been ridden double before. I could feel him getting ready to buck, but the girl said "Blue!" in a tone I wouldn't have argued with, either, and booted him in the ribs. We took off at a gallop.

Even in the half-dark I could see Angel's white mane and tail from a long way off. But not as soon as I could hear the sickening screech of wire being jerked.

We were still a hundred yards away when the girl pulled the roan down to a walk. At first I wondered what she was doing, but then I realized she was thinking straighter than I was. The fastest way to panic a scared horse is to ride up behind it at a dead gallop.

We were close enough to see the blood when she stopped the roan and handed me the halter. "She knows you. I'll stay here till you get hold of her."

Angel wasn't fighting the wire anymore. She was wrapped up so tight she could hardly move. Blood and sweat trickled down her legs onto the ground. She was shivering all over.

"Whoa, Angel," I said softly. My voice didn't sound like me. "Easy girl." I moved closer. She snorted and tried to back up. A loop of wire tightened around her rump, and she went crazy again.

She tried everything. She reared and kicked and fought, but the barbs just sawed deeper. Suddenly she gathered all her muscles and jumped. The wire screeched, and I prayed she'd break loose. But she didn't. The wire held, and she fell heavily on her side. She couldn't get up.

I knelt on the ground beside her. "Please, girl, just lay still. Easy girl. You're gonna be okay." She didn't move as I slipped the halter over her head.

Then the girl was beside me with the wire cutter in her hand. "Where do we start?" she whispered.

"I don't know," I said, holding out my hand for the cutter. "You hold her head. I'll cut the wire." I had a feeling that somebody was going to get cut up before we were done, and I didn't want it to be her. She handed it over. It was going to be dark soon, and I had to start somewhere, so I cut the wires that weren't too tight first. As I did I could see that most of the cuts were messy but not deep. Angel's chest was laid open in a couple of places, but I'd seen lots of horses with cuts like that, and they had healed fast.

Behind me I could hear the girl talking baby talk to Angel. It didn't make any sense, but it was sure working. Between talking and rubbing behind her ears she had that horse practically hypnotized.

"That's real good. Just keep talking to her like that," I said over my shoulder. Then I realized that I still didn't even know who I was talking to. "Well, what is your name, anyhow?" It was out before I thought about it sounding like I was mad at her or something.

She didn't even look up, but I saw a half-smile cross her face. "Casey Sutherland," she said. Her tone of voice didn't change. She probably thought you talked to crazy horses and confused kids the same way.

I had all the wires loose, I thought. Then Angel shifted a little, and I heard the twang of wire again. It was her hind leg, the underneath one. The wire was around the hock joint and worked in so deep it was out of sight. One end was still fastened to an old post, and the other end was buried in the mud. If I cut either end, the tension from the other was going to jerk the wire out of the horse's leg, and she was going to go straight up.

"You better get out of the way," I said to Casey. "All hell's gonna bust loose when I cut this wire."

"Just do it." She didn't move.

I grabbed the wire with my right hand to take off as much tension as I could. That meant I'd have to cut the wire left-handed. Real handy. I jammed the jaws of the cutter together.

Everything happened at once. I heard the wire snap, felt something red-hot tear through my hand, and saw Angel's big body heaving upward above me. I rolled away from the scrambling hooves.

I opened my eyes a second later. Angel was on her feet, snorting and shaking. Casey was on the ground with mud all over her, but she was still holding on to the halter rope.

She didn't move as I got up and eased over to Angel. "I've got her," I said, and Casey let go of the rope and slowly stood up.

"You okay?" I asked.

"Yeah. Are you?"

"Yeah," I said. About then I noticed my hand was bleeding some, but it wasn't bad, so I shoved it in my jeans pocket.

Casey walked slowly around Angel. "The back leg's bad. I'd better get my mother."

"Your mother?"

"Yeah. She's a vet. Our place is next to yours, and her clinic's there. Try and lead the horse down to the barn, where there's some light. We'll meet you there."

I heard the roan's hoofbeats fade away up the hill.

Every step seemed like forever. I didn't think Angel would make it down to the barn. And I wasn't sure I wanted her to. The way that leg was dragging, I was afraid she was walking to a mercy killing.

The lights were on in the barn, and a van was parked outside.

Casey's mom was blond, too, but kind of faded and gray-streaked. She was a lot older than I'd expected her to be, and she looked really tired. She hardly noticed me as she started sweet-talking Angel, running her hands over her neck and shoulders, gradually working her way back to the hind leg.

"Bring that light over here so I can get a good look, Casey," she ordered.

Casey shone the light right on the wound, and I got a good look, too. I also just about got sick. Through the shredded flesh and oozing blood the light caught the dull white gleam of bone. I turned away and leaned my face against Angel's neck, wishing I was dead.

Mrs. Sutherland sighed. "Well, there's a chance. Anyway, I can't put her down without the owner's consent, so we might as well try."

She seemed to be telling, not asking, so I didn't say anything. There wasn't much to say anyway.

She gave Angel a couple of needles that calmed her down a lot. Then she went to work, cleaning, cutting, and sewing. She did the surface cuts first. She just put some kind of salve on most of them, but she put a couple of stitches in Angel's chest. "This would heal all right without the stitches, but they'll cut down on the scarring," she said.

That made me start hoping. Scars on a permanently crippled—or dead—horse don't matter much.

Then she started on the leg. She probed around in the cut for a while. Then she looked up. "Well, you can thank God the tendons aren't cut. If they were gone . . ." She didn't need to finish that sentence.

She worked on the leg for a long time. Finally she wrapped the whole joint in some kind of stretchy bandage and straightened up slowly, as if her back hurt. "That's about it. Now all we can do is wait and see."

"Will she get better?" I asked. I must have sounded about six years old, but I couldn't help it.

Mrs. Sutherland smiled, a tired, sad kind of a smile that made me think she'd been asked that question a lot of times and that the answers had never been easy. "No promises, kid—but I've seen some pretty hopeless cases fool the experts."

I guess I must have looked about six right then, too, because suddenly she put her arm around me and gave me a big hug. I'd never been hugged by a vet before, but it sure felt good. "Don't give up on her yet. She's got good stuff in her."

Then, before I had time to digest that, she swooped down like a hawk and grabbed my wrist. "What's this?"

she demanded. I'd forgotten all about the cut on my
hand. It didn't hurt much, but it had bled enough to
make a real mess.

I shrugged. "Got tangled up while I was cutting the
wire off her."

"Hand me the disinfectant, Casey."

It was the same stuff she had used on the horse, and it
sure was horse-strength. I couldn't help trying to jerk my
hand back, but it didn't matter. She was used to holding
thousand-pound horses, and I don't think she even noticed. So I stood there sweating while she cleaned the cut
out good.

"Well, you'll have to go to a doctor for a tetanus shot."
She grinned. "My needles weren't designed for scrawny
kids."

"I just had a tetanus shot a couple of months ago." It
was at the last school I'd gone to. I got there just in time
for tetanus shots, fluoride treatments, the where-babies-
come-from films (they must think kids don't watch the
soap operas), and Fire Prevention Week. By the time they
got around to schoolwork, we were moving on again.

Mrs. Sutherland didn't give up easily. "Okay, but I
think I'd better run you in for a couple of stitches anyway."

"No!" I hadn't planned to say it quite that way, but it
just came out. I was feeling bad enough without replaying that old scene from the past. About then she noticed
the scar on my hand and gave me a curious look, like she
was going to start asking questions. *Please, not now,* I
thought. It must have shown on my face because she
suddenly shrugged and turned to Casey. "Okay, if that's
the way it's going to be, hand me a horse bandage. I
guess it'll work just as well on a mule."

It was getting late by the time she loaded all her stuff in the van, but tired as she was, she stopped in the doorway, looking worried. "Are you sure you'll be okay here alone until your dad gets home?"

A lot better than I'll be after he gets home, I thought, but I just nodded.

"Well, okay. You can try feeding her, but don't worry if she isn't interested. She won't starve. I'll come down tomorrow to check the bandage, and my number's in the book if you need me."

"Thanks," I said. It didn't seem like enough, but that was all there was to say.

She went out, and I could hear her arranging her stuff in the back of the van.

That left Casey and me. Up in the pasture with Angel it had seemed like we'd known each other forever. Now we were suddenly strangers again. We stood there looking at each other. Then she turned and patted Angel's neck. "Take it easy, girl," she said softly and turned to walk away.

That's it? I thought. *She says good-bye to the horse and leaves?*

Suddenly she stopped and turned toward me. "I'm really sorry, Shane," she said, almost in a whisper. She was looking right at me, and the light from the bare bulb caught her face. I could have sworn there were tears in her eyes. I know girls are supposed to cry easy, but over a horse that didn't even belong to her? It was crazy.

But I guess I like crazy people because right then she became the most special girl in the world to me.

She had turned away and was almost at the door. "Casey!" I almost yelled it. She stopped and looked back, but her face was in the shadows now. I couldn't let her go without saying something, so I said the first thing that came into my head. "Your mom's real nice!"

I know it was stupid, but the only other thing I could think of was "I love you," and I didn't think she was quite ready to hear that.

"Thanks," she said, in kind of a funny tone. "See you tomorrow."

Then she was gone.

7

I watched the lights of the van until they disappeared. Then silence and darkness settled over the valley, giving me that funny feeling I get sometimes if I wake up late at night. The feeling that I must be the only person left in the whole world.

I looked at my watch. It was five after eleven. I couldn't believe that today had been just one day. It seemed like I'd had enough trouble for at least a week.

The other horses had followed Angel back to the barn, so I shut them back into the corral. Then I got Angel some of that precious hay I'd been so proud of saving. Oh, yeah, I'd saved some hay, all right. And practically killed a horse to do it. I should have known there was a reason Dad hadn't let the horses into that pasture. I should have waited. . . . But all the *should have*'s in the world weren't going to change things. They weren't going to give me another chance. Nothing was going to change the way Dad was going to feel. It wasn't going to change the way I felt either.

I put my arms around Angel's neck and buried my face

in her mane. "I'm sorry, girl," I whispered. Then, maybe it was because I didn't know how I was going to face Dad, or maybe because I was so tired, or maybe I'd just had more than I could take in one day, but the next thing I knew I was crying. Bawling like a baby, in spite of all my mom had taught me about being brave. And I'd thought girls cried easy. . . .

It took a long time to get all cried out. Finally I raised my head and wiped my face on my sleeve. I took a deep breath and swallowed hard. I could taste salt. They say that tears are salty, but then again so is horse sweat.

In all the stories I've read, crying's supposed to make you feel better. Well, it doesn't. It just made my sore ribs ache and left me feeling kind of drained. And cold. Even leaning against Angel's warm body, I was shivering. It may have been the beginning of summer, but this was Alberta.

I knew if I didn't lie down soon, I was going to be out on my feet, so I thought about going to bed. But I knew I wouldn't sleep, so I grabbed a horse blanket and bedded down in the corner of the stall to wait for Dad. I would rather have waited to face a firing squad than have to tell him that I'd probably destroyed that horse. Mom's horse.

I was wrong about not sleeping. The next thing I knew, I was waking up, cold and stiff, and confused. At first I thought I was in bed and the radio was on. Then I realized that nobody who sang that bad could get on the radio.

I hadn't heard Dad sing "Me and Bobby McGee" for a long time. He must be either pretty drunk or pretty happy. Then I remembered why I was sleeping in the barn, and I knew he wasn't going to stay either way very long.

Jeff's voice broke in. "Hey, there's lights on in the barn."

I was still trying to get the kinks out of my muscles and the straw out of my hair when they walked into the barn. They didn't even see me at first, back there in the shadows. But they saw Angel.

For all Dad's bad habits he doesn't swear much. Maybe Mom broke him of it the same way she did me. I used to blow bubbles for a week from the soap in my mouth every time I tried out a new word.

But Dad swore now, and it wasn't one of his Irish-temper outbursts. It was low-voiced and cold.

Then he turned and saw me. He didn't say a word, at first. He just stood there looking at me with eyes like a cornered wildcat's, except they were blue instead of yellow.

I made myself look back into those eyes, but it was the hardest thing I've ever done. "We were running out of hay, so I let the horses out," I said. I was surprised at how steady my voice sounded. I sure didn't feel steady. "She got tangled up in an old falling-down wire fence that I didn't know was there."

I almost added "I'm sorry," but something stopped me. I don't know what. Maybe that famous Morgan pride. God only knew I was sorrier than I'd ever been for anything I'd done in my life, but I just couldn't say it. Not to Dad. Not when he was looking at me like that. Blaming me because I'd messed up something he should have been doing himself—would have been doing if he hadn't been sneaking off to a rodeo instead. So I just glared back at him.

He still didn't say anything, but I could hear him breathing clear across the stall. His hands were knotted into fists, and I thought he was going to hit me. I almost hoped he would. It might make me feel better.

He didn't hit me. But the words he finally said hurt a whole lot more. "I should've known better than to trust you with *her* horse." His voice was so hard and cold, I started shivering again. He spun around and slammed his fist against the wall and walked out into the night.

Jeff had been standing back, staying out of it, but now he heaved himself away from the wall he was leaning on and pushed his hat back so I could see his face. "C'mon, kid, standin' out here freezin' to death ain't gonna help nothin'."

I didn't move.

"Hey, Short Stuff, snap out of it. It ain't the end of the world."

He reached out and put his big, hairy, grizzly-bear arm around my shoulders. The way things had been going, you'd think I'd have grabbed for a little affection like an orphan pup. But it wasn't Jeff's affection I wanted.

I jerked loose. "Leave me alone, Jeff! I ain't your kid, and I don't have to jump every time you holler."

"Listen, Shane . . ." Jeff started, his voice sounding like he was talking to a spooked horse.

"Listen to what? Listen to some more of your lies? Where's the horse you went to Cochrane to buy?"

I don't know what I was trying to do. Nobody had ever been a better friend to me than Jeff, but I felt good when the look that crossed his face told me I'd scored a hurting shot.

"You're a phony, Jeff. A big, irresponsible phony. Just like my old man's a useless, fallin'-down-drunk clown." I never had a chance to figure out where I'd heard those last few words before because all I saw was a blur as Jeff's big hand shot out and grabbed me by the front of my jacket. He threw me against the wall so hard my teeth rattled.

"Quit it, Shane!" His voice cut through me like a whip.

Time seemed to hang frozen as he stood there, towering over me. Slowly I looked up, trying to read his face. Most of the anger had already faded. He looked different from the Jeff I thought I knew. Older. And sadder.

Then he started talking, slow and quiet. "Did you see this horse when she was tangled up in the wire?"

I nodded.

"All right. Then, tell me, did she get cut up so bad because she got tangled up or because she wouldn't quit fightin', no matter how bad it hurt her?"

I didn't know what he was driving at, but I wasn't about to get sassy again. I shrugged. "Fighting, I guess."

Jeff nodded. "That's right. And the same thing happens to people. Life sometimes tangles you up real bad. And you've only got two choices. Live with it as best you can and try and untangle it a little at a time. Or be like this poor ol' horse. Tear yourself to pieces fightin' it and still not get loose."

He was quiet a minute, and when he started talking again, he sounded tired. "And you Morgans are real good at tearing yourselves up."

He stopped talking then, and the late night country quiet settled around us.

It seemed like a long time later when he spoke again, low, hardly breaking that silence. "You understand what I'm tryin' to tell you, kid?"

"Yeah, Jeff, I understand." I sighed. "I'm a fighter, not

an untangler. But I think I'm about finished fighting for tonight."

"Good. Then let's go in before we freeze plumb to death."

His arm around me felt good as we walked across the dew-wet grass to the house.

8

The alarm clock was dead, and it had been after one in the morning when I finally hit the sack, so I didn't expect to wake up until noon. But I surprised myself. It was just a little after six, and already sunshine was pouring in through my window. I groaned and rolled over, feeling like something the cat had dragged in. I wanted so bad to go back to sleep, but I had too much on my mind. The harder I tried, the wider awake I got.

Finally I gave up and staggered over to the mirror to check the situation out. Yeah, I *looked* like something the cat had dragged in, too.

I must have been really wiped out when I fell into bed last night. I hadn't even bothered to wash the top layer of dirt off. On top of the cuts and bruises from the fight my face was muddy from wrestling with Angel out in the pasture, and the whole mess was streaky from bawling all over it. Wow, was I pretty! Move over, Scott Baio, the newest teenage idol has arrived!

At least the black eye hadn't swelled much after all. In fact, my eyes were about the only part of me that looked like they were still alive. They're real blue, like Dad's. That's about all of his looks I got, thank goodness. The rest of me looks more like Mom did.

I supposed maybe I needed a haircut. It was getting kind of hard to see out. But I usually resist having my ears lowered until somebody starts asking if I'm the new girl. I really hate haircuts.

I tried running a comb through that jungle and soon found out my hand was still sore. I looked at it and saw that Mrs. Sutherland's nice, white horse bandage was dirty already. I just about took it off, but I remembered she was coming back, and I was afraid maybe she'd get out the horse disinfectant again if she thought I'd got the cut dirty. I left the bandage alone.

I'm not usually overly fond of water, unless I'm swimming, but this was one time nobody needed to convince me that a shower would be a good idea. Besides, it would be a good way to postpone something I didn't want to face.

I stayed in the shower till the water went cold and my toes wrinkled. "Okay, Mr. Clean," I told myself at last, "you can quit stalling. You're gonna have to find out, sooner or later."

I found some clean clothes and walked out of the house into the morning.

There's something about early morning sunshine that makes it almost impossible to stay feeling really bad. I sure didn't have much to look forward to this morning, but just walking to the barn made me feel better than I'd thought I could ever feel again.

Still, I lifted up the latch on the barn door like I was defusing a live grenade. I didn't know what was waiting for me.

I opened the door . . . and froze in my tracks. Angel was not only still on her feet, but she had her ears pointed my way, and she was nickering at me in that soft but demanding way that means a horse wants something, and wants it right now.

She still looked pretty rough, and she wasn't putting hardly any weight on that leg, but she sure looked better than she'd looked last night.

"Hey, how you doin', you poor old wreck?" I asked, giving her a scratch behind the ears. She shook her head impatiently. A scratch behind the ears wasn't what she had in mind.

"You hungry?" She didn't say anything, so I decided it was worth a try. I went and got the oat bucket.

She heard it rattle as I picked it up and started hollering at me again. She even took a couple of steps toward me, about as fast as a wounded turtle, but she could walk.

She almost knocked the bucket out of my hand when I tried to pour some oats into the feedbox. Then she started eating, and the steady crunch-grind of her chomping on those oats had to be the world's most beautiful sound.

Suddenly I got that being-watched feeling on the back of my neck. I turned, slow and careful, and there was old Jeff. He was leaning against the door, grinning his grizzly-bear grin in a way that said *See, I tried to tell you it wasn't the end of the world.* But he had enough class not to say *I told you so* out loud, so I grinned back.

"Want me to warm you up the chili for breakfast?" he asked innocently.

I punched him, and he dangled me off the ground in the usual bear hug. Things were back to normal—almost. But when he'd set me down and I'd got my wind back, I couldn't help asking, "Is Dad up yet?"

Jeff's grin faded a little. "No, I don't think he'll be up for a while. . . ." He looked like he was going to say some more, but I didn't give him the chance.

"Yeah, you don't have to explain. I understand. Things got kind of rough last night, so he had some of his favorite pain-killer. And now he ain't feeling any pain." I was the only one that laughed, and my laugh sounded sort of hollow. "You know, Jeff," I went on, mainly because I couldn't get stopped, "I'll sure be glad when I'm old enough to start drinking, so when things go wrong—"

"Shane, cut it out." Jeff's warning tone stopped me right there.

I knew I should have left the subject alone. "I have to get ready for school," I said and got out of there before I managed to get Jeff mad again.

I didn't care who stared at me on the bus this time. I had to talk to Casey, so when I got on the bus, I just kept walking back there.

Casey looked at me like she thought I was one brick short of a load. "Well, aren't you going to move over so I can sit down and be inconspicuous?" I asked. I liked that word. I learned it from a teacher I had once. She always used to say, "Shane, if you would just try to make yourself inconspicuous." She usually said it when I did something like fall out of my desk trying to get my pencil I'd dropped. My balance is much better on a horse than in a desk.

Anyway, Casey finally moved over, but I noticed she was blushing. My face felt kind of warm, too.

I sat down beside her and looked up, right into that big

mirror they have at the front of school buses, and right into the puzzled eyes of the driver. Well, I've seen enough poker games to know that if you're going to bluff, bluff good, so I smiled up at him like I knew what I was doing, and never blinked. It seemed a long time later when he kind of shrugged and ground the gears as he pulled into the road.

Just then the worried voice of my friend in the front seat carried over all the normal bus noise. "Hey, Shane! You're in the wrong seat!"

"Quiet down, Alvin," said the driver, bless him.

Then I turned to Casey. "She's better. She was real hungry this morning, and she can walk a little, too."

Suddenly I noticed that every kid on the bus was turned around, taking it all in. I guess I was talking kind of loud. I hadn't learned to be inconspicuous, after all.

But Casey didn't seem to mind. "That's great, Shane! Mom said she'd wait till after school to check on her so I could come along." She stopped and hesitated a minute, like she wasn't sure she should say anything more, but then she asked, real quietly, "Did your dad get home?"

I nodded.

"What did he say?"

I was almost mad at her for asking that. Sometimes my problems with Dad felt like a knife sticking in me. I could live with the pain of them just being there, but let anybody jar them a little and watch out!

But Casey wasn't just anybody, so I tried to make it sound halfway like a joke when I said "Don't ask!"

From the look she gave me, I guess it didn't sound even half-joking. I could tell she sensed something was wrong, and I wished she knew the whole story, but I didn't think I'd ever be able to tell it to her.

"I think Alvin's missing you," Casey said with a grin. "See you at school."

I moved up to my old seat. Alvin gave me a stern look.

"I thought you'd be back. It's actually much more comfortable up here. Besides, nobody wants to sit with a girl."

That's a matter of opinion, Alvin.

9

We had language first thing. Miss Bradley was handing back spelling tests we'd done the day before. She saved mine till last. I hoped that was a coincidence.

"Shane?"

I walked up to her desk, and she held out my paper. I was relieved to see an 88 percent on it. "You're a very good speller," she said.

I grinned. She wasn't bad-looking, for a teacher.

I started to leave, but she was still holding on to the paper. "However," she went on, and I didn't like the sound of the *however*, "it did take me the better part of the night to translate your handwriting into English."

I was starting to get embarrassed, and when I'm embarrassed, I can do some really stupid things. I looked down at the paper. My writing looked normal to me. I could read it okay. Then I caught a glimpse of my bandaged hand, and I suddenly got this brilliant idea of how to get Miss Bradley off my case. I'd run across a few teachers that would fall for anything once, so I thought it was worth a try.

"Yeah, well, I'm sorry about the mess, but you see, I got kind of cut up, and it really hurts to write." I gave her my best puppy-dog look. If I played my cards right, I might get out of today's work, too.

I could see that I had her concerned. "What happened?" she asked.

"Oh, I got it caught in some barbed wire trying to get a horse untangled." I almost got carried away and started telling her about how it should have had stitches and everything, but I caught myself in time. *Watch it, stupid! You'll soon be winning yourself an all-expenses-paid trip to the nurse.*

But I had Miss Bradley softened up. She was really sympathetic. "That's too bad, Shane. I'm sure it does hurt." Then she got this kind of funny look on her face as she added, "And when did you say this happened?"

"Last n—" I started, but the word kind of died. I had just cooked my goose. "Last night," I finished weakly.

She shook her head, and still in that sympathetic tone she said, "Well, that really is too bad, Shane." Then she raised one eyebrow. "And to think it's a retroactive cut at that."

"Retroactive?" I said. I didn't know what it meant, but it sounded serious.

"Well, if it didn't happen till last night but it affected yesterday afternoon's work, it must be retroactive." The look on her face said, *Your move, kid.*

Well, even I am smart enough to know when I'm licked. "Yeah, well, uh, I guess I'd better try and be neater next time, huh?"

"That's what I had in mind," she said, grinning.

Finally I got to sit down. It was still first period, but I'd already learned something. Miss Bradley was not one of the teachers who fall for anything once. But I liked her. I don't mind so much when teachers win, as long as they do it with a little class.

She gave us some dictionary exercises next, and I made it a point to look up *retroactive.* I had a feeling it was going to join *inconspicuous* in my personal vocabulary.

The next period was math. I wasn't looking forward to any more intersections, but I settled in my desk and prepared to endure.

Greg Jacobs, the kid behind me, poked me in the back. I turned around. "Hey, Shane, did you get all that homework done?"

"What homew—" I started. Then, for the first time since yesterday afternoon, those eight pages of math crossed my mind. "Not exactly," I said with a groan. "You think Mr. Thorpe will settle for half of it?"

Greg laughed. "Thorpe? You gotta be kidding! He'll have you in detention for a week if he doesn't decide to send you to Petersen to explain why you didn't get it done."

There wasn't time for suicide. Mr. Thorpe walked in and slammed the door behind him. He wasn't in the world's greatest mood.

He started right in intersecting, and it was so boring, I just about dropped off to sleep. Still, I wasn't complaining. He seemed to have forgotten about the homework.

About halfway through the period he stopped talking and assigned some questions. I was being more inconspicuous than I'd ever thought was possible. But I felt his gaze settle on me. "Oh, yes, Shawn" (I hate that!), "I'll be there in a minute to go over your homework."

Just as I was prepared for instant death, somebody

asked him a question. While he was answering that the intercom suddenly crackled to life, and the secretary came on. "Please excuse the interruption, but all those wishing to participate in the cross-country are to assemble at the starting line immediately."

"What's the cross-country?" I asked anyone who was listening.

"Two miles of torture!" answered the fat kid across the aisle. He sounded like he really meant it.

Greg pointed out the window. "See that big hill?" I could hardly miss it. It filled the whole horizon. "You run over the top of it and back again."

"Run up it?" I asked. It looked like a big enough job just to climb it.

"Sure. You get used to it. Deer Valley's got the best cross-country runners in the province because they train on that hill." He picked up his books. "You coming?"

Well, it was either a week of noon hours sweating over that math book or half an hour of sweating over the hill. Fortunately I'm not as stupid as I look. . . .

"Wouldn't miss it," I said.

These kids were either the world's most dedicated jocks or the world's greatest math-haters. About three quarters of the class went out. I noticed Casey was one of them.

I followed the crowd to the bottom of the hill. Most of the kids seemed to take this real seriously, and they were stripped down to shorts and school T-shirts. We hadn't had phys. ed. yet since I'd come, so nobody had told me we had to have shorts, and I wasn't about to get some voluntarily. I feel like a fool running around with my bony knees sticking out.

I'd been wearing my running shoes when we went out

to untangle Angel, and they were still soaking wet this morning, so I'd worn my riding boots to school. Tight blue jeans, a cowboy shirt, and boots. That was going to be a great outfit for running over this mountain. Still, it was better than math. Anything was better than math.

We were standing around, waiting for them to get the show on the road, when I noticed that the fat kid was out here, too. From what he'd said about running, I thought he'd have stuck with math. "Hey, Pete!" I yelled to him. "Did you change your mind?"

He laughed. "No way! I don't run unless something big is chasing me! Mr. Thorpe decided that since most of the class was gone, the rest of us could come and watch. It happens like that every year, but the teachers always pretend that the ones that don't run will have to work. They get great participation that way!"

What a rip-off! If I'd stayed cool for another few minutes, I'd have got out of math anyway. But now I'd gone and signed up.

I never have liked school sports much. Not that I've been in one school long enough to get really involved in them. But compared to something like steer riding, volleyball has never seemed like a high-tension sport. And, to tell the truth, I'm too independent to like team sports. When I make a mistake, I don't want to hear about it from a dozen other guys. It's bad enough hearing about it from myself. So if I had to get involved in something, I guess I couldn't have picked a more individual sport than running.

I guessed I could run as well as the next guy. At least I'd had enough practice at it. Sometimes, when we were camped at a rodeo ground somewhere, we'd let the horses out in a field overnight. And sure enough, in the

morning, when I was in a hurry to catch him, Reb would
remember his sense of humor again. I'd get him almost
cornered, and suddenly he'd give this funny little whinny
that sounded more like a laugh and take off again, leaving me in the dust. So I'd get to run around the field a
couple more times.

Eventually either Reb would give up or Dad would get
tired of waiting, pick up the halter, and walk right
straight up to that rotten horse and put it on. Then, every
time, just like a recording, Dad would grin at me and say,
"I keep tellin' you, kid. You're never gonna be able to
outrun this horse. You gotta outsmart him." I didn't like
his sense of humor any better than Reb's.

Even after we left the horses at Jeff's, I was still always
running somewhere. It seems like, around a rodeo, any
kid running loose automatically becomes everybody's
gofer. You know what I mean. "Shane, will you just go fer
a hamburger for me over at the concession stand?" Or "I
forgot my rope over in my truck"—parked at the other
end of the rodeo grounds half a mile away. "Just run and
get it, will you, kid?"

Yeah, I could run all right, when I had to. But that kind
of running had some purpose to it. Running up this hill
in a cloud of dust with a whole herd of other guys just to
see who got back first didn't turn me on. Pete sure had
the right idea.

Speaking of Pete, he had wandered over, and now he
was eyeing my boots. "You gonna run in those?"

"Yeah, that's all I got."

"What size running shoes do you wear?"

"Sevens."

"Close enough. These are eights." He sat down and started untying them. As long as he didn't have to do the running, Pete was the cross-country's biggest promoter. I sure hoped he didn't have his shorts handy, too.

10

The coach was giving instructions about the race into a loudspeaker. "Now, as you know, the route will be clearly marked by red flags, over Snake Hill. . . ."

"How'd it get that name?" I asked the guy next to me.

He looked at me like I was crazy. " 'Cause of the snakes," he said.

"Really? There's snakes up there?"

"Hundreds of 'em."

Where I come from, *snake* means *rattler*. This whole crazy school must have a unanimous death wish.

"There's hundreds of rattlers up there where we're running?" I squeaked.

He laughed. "Rattlers? Never seen one in my life. Garters."

"Oh."

They called our class then. The coach was walking up and down, looking us over. He stopped in front of me, looking like he'd just discovered an extraterrestrial. "You new here?"

"Yeah."

"I thought so." I don't think he was impressed with my track suit. So I rolled up my sleeves. Maybe that would help.

The gun went off for the girls' race, and they were off. I tried to see Casey, but at that distance they all looked the same. Except for one. A girl with curly black hair and a red track suit was already so far ahead that I would have laid odds on her to win, right from the start.

Then we lined up. The gun went. The start was more like a cattle stampede than a race, with about thirty of us all taking off at the same time. No one seemed too worried about it, though. If you get a bad start, you've got two miles to make up for it.

Well, since I'd got involved in this thing strictly by accident, I wasn't planning on busting myself over it, so I started out at an easy jog that kept me somewhere in the middle of the pack.

I was still there when the trail narrowed and started to climb. I could hear somebody coming up behind me. Then, as we rounded a bend, I could feel him pull up beside me. *So go, if you're in such a hurry.* I moved over a little.

Suddenly a big elbow smashed me in the ribs. "Outta my way, punk!" growled a familiar voice. I got a glimpse of a swollen nose with a Band-Aid across it. Bart Willard. Just who I'd always wanted to go jogging with. I must really be a slow learner because, in spite of what had happened yesterday, I would have liked to try round two, right there and then.

But he was already out of reach, gaining ground on a slight downgrade. Seeing him in his track suit, I had to admit that, as well as being big, the guy was in pretty good shape. But he wasn't as good as he thought he was. Nobody could be that good.

Before I knew it, I was putting on a little speed, really starting to push it. I wasn't gaining on him, but I wasn't losing anymore either. We passed five or six guys on that downgrade. I was starting to sweat.

Then the trail started uphill again. *Come on, Bart, slow down. You can't keep up this pace uphill.* He kept it up. I saw him glance over his shoulder once, and he looked kind of surprised.

We passed another couple of guys. I was getting a side ache, and I could hear Bart wheezing like a wind-broken horse. There were teachers stationed here and there along the trail. Probably supposed to bring back the bodies of the ones who didn't make it. One of the teachers hollered as we went by, "Nice run, boys! You've made the halfway mark!"

Halfway! I must have run at least four miles already! Bart was widening the space a little. The trail went into a steeper uphill pitch. I undid a couple more buttons on my shirt and pulled it out of my jeans. I just about took it off and left it there, but that would mean having to come back for it. I'd rather have died of heat exhaustion than have to climb that hill again.

We were almost at the top now. The rest of the course spread out below us. Where was everybody? I could only count two runners ahead of Bart. I recognized the front one. Somebody had pointed him out to me. He was a provincial champ or something, and he looked it. He was running like he was still enjoying it. I hated him for that. The other runner at least had the decency to look miserable.

I was close enough behind Bart now to see the sweat

soaking the back of his T-shirt. But he wasn't slowing down any. I couldn't believe that anyone that big and heavy could keep up that pace.

I was getting dizzy and starting to see red stars, but Bart passed another kid, so I passed the kid, too. Bart glanced over his shoulder and speeded up a little. I speeded up a little.

The first-place guy crossed the finish line about one hundred yards ahead of us. My side was hurting so much I was holding it with my hand as I ran. I started to ease up a little, but a sudden memory swept me back to the last National Finals Dad had ridden in. Halfway through that week a bull had fallen on him in the chute. Dad had come out of that wreck with three broken ribs and a dislocated shoulder. But he didn't give up. He'd gone on and ridden four more bulls that week . . . and won the championship. Whatever else my dad was, he wasn't a quitter. If he could take that kind of pain, I knew I could take a little more, too. I don't know if it was because I hated him or because I loved him, but I do know that it was thinking about Dad that gave me guts enough to finish that race. And once I'd decided to hang in there, I also remembered who I had to thank for those sore ribs, and I got mad. Maybe I couldn't outfight Bart, but I was going to outrun him. I moved up beside him, and I could see by his face that he was finished.

"Outta my way, punk!" I gasped and passed him. Three more strides and I fell across the finish line and lay there, hugging the ground and absorbing its coolness, trying to remember how to breathe.

Then some teacher was dragging me to my feet. "Come on, son. Get up and walk. If you cool off too fast, you'll get sick."

I half-expected him to throw a blanket on me and give
me a rubdown. Like a horse . . . As soon as I thought
horse, a picture of Angel tearing herself up in that wire
flashed into my mind. I wondered how I had managed to
stop thinking about her for this long. What was happening at home now? How was Angel doing? And Dad—
what was he thinking? I remembered that scene in the
barn last night, and a sudden shiver ran through me.

"See, you're already getting chilled." The teacher was
flapping around me like a disturbed setting hen. I managed to kind of shake him off and walk around on my
own, getting my breathing back to normal and my mind
back to the present.

People kept congratulating me. I don't know why.
Number two has never been famous for anything except
trying harder. But I guess the number one guy was so
good that seeing him win was no big deal anymore. He
came over and talked to me. For a superjock he was a nice
kid.

Then I almost walked right into good old Bart. He was
stumbling around, looking about as wiped-out as I felt.
We looked at each other, and then—the devil must have
made me do it, because I grinned at him and said,
"Those cigarettes'll get you every time, Bart."

His face was worth seeing. I think he almost started to
laugh. I also think he almost slugged me. I walked away
before he could make a choice.

The coach spotted me then and pounced like a tiger
scenting fresh blood. "Hey, I want to talk to you! What's
your name?"

I told him.

"Well, you just ran that race in only fifteen seconds
longer than it took Jim Nelson, and he's rated in the top

five in the province. And you did it without training and wearing those"—his eyes swept over me as if there was something indecent about jeans—"those blue jeans. Do you realize what that means?"

Yeah, if I'm not careful, for a reward I'll get to keep doing this until I drop dead, I thought. I decided that just "No" was a safer answer, though.

"What it means . . ." There was a long pause, and I could see he was trying to remember my name. If he called me Shawn, he'd never get me to run across the street for him. But he made it. "It means, Shane, that you are a natural runner, and with proper training you can go a long way."

Yeah, a long way up and down that stinking hill. I didn't say that out loud either. I didn't say anything.

"So," he went on, "practice is every day at noon. Show up here tomorrow, with your shorts." He stressed the last part. Then he looked me up and down and added, "And try a smaller size running shoe. Your toes are curling up."

I'd almost forgotten I had Pete's shoes on. I'd better find him before he had to go home in his socks. I was just about to use that excuse to escape from the coach when a girl's voice called, "Hey, Shane! Great run!" I turned around. It was the black-haired girl. The one who had come in first in the girls' race. "I'm Cheryl Anderson. We'll both get to run in the South-Central Zone Championships in a couple of weeks. Maybe we can get in some practice together."

Zone Championships? Practice? She said it like those were the greatest events of the year. And I figured this running was about as much fun as banging your head on the wall. It feels real good when you stop.

But with a girl like Cheryl Anderson standing there smiling at me, it was hard to remember that. "Yeah, well, sure," I said.

"Good. See you at noon tomorrow." She left, and I caught a glimpse of the smile on the coach's face. I felt like a mouse who'd just reached for the cheese. . . .

I found Pete and then hung around with him and some other guys from our class, watching the high school races. Eventually we kind of drifted into a group with some of the girls. Casey was there, so I got a chance to talk to her without making a big deal of it. I didn't want to embarrass her by hanging around her like we were going steady or something. Some girls seem to like having their own private boyfriend following them around like a tame colt, but I didn't think Casey was that type of girl. And I didn't think I'd like to be halter-broke either.

She and a couple of her friends came over to me. "That was a fantastic race, Shane," she said. She really meant it, too. Casey never says something just because it's what's expected. That's one of the things I liked about her.

"Thanks. How'd you do?"

"Oh, about tenth, I think. I'm no great runner, but it helps your phys. ed. mark if you participate."

From what I'd seen, Casey didn't need help with any of her marks. She was the best in the class in every subject we'd had.

"Tenth is pretty good out of that many," I said.

She smiled. She has a real nice smile.

11

Casey waved to me as I watched the bus roar on up the hill. I turned and walked slowly toward the house. It had been another crazy day. I hadn't even had time to think. I was glad, because now that I did have time, I didn't like my thoughts much.

I started wondering about Angel. And that started me remembering last night. I didn't know how much longer this Mexican standoff between Dad and me was going to last, but I did know it was like living under a high-tension wire that could snap at any minute.

Then I noticed that Jeff's truck was in the yard, but this time Dad's was missing. This was starting out like an instant replay of last night. And that was one movie I did not want to see again.

I went in the house and threw my books on a chair. Sure enough, there was another note on the table. This time in Jeff's writing.

In town bying gr̶a̶s̶s̶ g̶e̶r̶o̶c̶ g̶r̶o̶c̶ grub.

Back soon

I couldn't help laughing. Now, there would be a chal-
lenge for Miss Bradley. But even while I was laughing I
was half-wondering if they'd heard there was a rodeo
somewhere around.

I also wondered where the grocery money was coming
from. Probably Jeff. The way I figured it, Dad must be
about broke. Having our own place was great, but it
didn't pay the bills. If Dad and I ever got to talking to
each other again, maybe I'd find out what he was planning to do for money.

Suddenly, out of nowhere, a thought that made grocery money seem like nothing crossed my mind. The vet
bill! A job like that could easily be worth a hundred
bucks, and she wasn't done yet. I got a sick feeling in the
bottom of my stomach. But I didn't have time to think
about it anymore. I heard the Sutherlands' van drive in.
They hadn't wasted any time. I went out to meet them.

"How's she doing?" Casey asked.

"I don't know. I haven't had time to look."

The three of us walked out to the barn.

Angel was too busy eating hay to give us more than a
casual flick of her ears. "She really is better!" Casey
whispered. Mrs. Sutherland didn't say anything, and I
couldn't read her face as she looked the horse over.

Outside in the yard a car door slammed, but I couldn't
take my eyes off Angel as Mrs. Sutherland unwrapped
the bandage on her leg. That lady sure could handle
horses. Angel barely twitched as she sponged the wound
out and rebandaged it.

At last she wiped her hands and turned to look at me.
At least I thought she was looking at me. But then I
realized she was looking behind me. I turned and saw
Dad and Jeff standing there.

For a minute nobody said anything, and all I could think of was those stupid lessons in manners they have in those old elementary school health books. You're supposed to introduce the gentlemen to the ladies first, I think. Gentlemen? Dad and Jeff? You gotta be kidding!

But just when I get my mind made up for sure about something, I turn out to be wrong. This time the something was Dad. He was sober as an owl and all cleaned up. He looked like everybody's idea of the gallant cowboy. He took his hat off and walked up to Casey's mother. "Ma'am, I'm Josh Morgan. The big fella under the hat is Jeff Burdette, and I guess you already know Shane." Before Mrs. Sutherland had a chance to answer, he went on, "I want to thank you for all you've done, takin' the trouble to come down here so late last night, and for the fine job you've done of fixin' this horse up. We really appreciate it."

Mrs. Sutherland smiled. "That's my job," she said, but I could see she was impressed with Dad. I was, too. I'd almost forgotten what a nice guy he could be sometimes.

There was a long silence then. Everyone was waiting for the answer, but no one wanted to ask the question. Finally Mrs. Sutherland answered it anyway. "Well, I can't promise you a Kentucky Derby winner. There's a lot of muscle damage, and some of it could be permanent." She paused and then smiled as she went on. "But barring any unforeseen complications, I think the least you can count on is a good, healthy broodmare."

That was like one of those old good news–bad news jokes, only it wasn't funny. Being a broodmare wasn't the future I'd had in mind for a horse like Angel. And I didn't dare even to think about how Dad would react to the idea. An electric silence hung in the air.

Then Dad smiled, a slow, sad smile, as he said, "Considering the way things looked last night, that sounds real good." He was looking at me, not her, when he said that, but I couldn't read what was on his mind.

Casey and I walked to their van together. I could see she was dying to tell me something. As soon as we got out of hearing of the others, she said, "You didn't tell me your dad was *that* Josh Morgan."

As far as I knew, I hadn't told her he was any Josh Morgan. "Huh?" I said.

"The champion bull rider."

I sighed. "That was a long time ago, Case. Ancient history."

"Yesterday is ancient history?"

"Casey," I said patiently, "what are you talking about?"

"The paper's in the van. See for yourself." She opened the door and brought out today's Calgary paper, opened to the sports section.

There it was in big, black letters.

A COMEBACK FOR MORGAN?

Spectators at yesterday's Cochrane rodeo were in for a special treat. Former North American Bull Riding Champion Josh Morgan demonstrated the style that has earned him that title twice. On a bull aptly named Amnesia he won the event with the almost unheard-of score of 88 points.

Morgan, who has not been riding for the past two or three years for what he terms "personal reasons," is now making his home in southern Alberta.

When asked why he picked Cochrane for a return to the sport, his reply was simply, "It was handy." He refused comment on whether this was the beginning of a bid to regain the championship.

I had to read it over twice before I could really take it in. So Dad had finally made that one big ride. The one he'd waited for for so long. No wonder he'd come home singing last night.

But he hadn't given me the chance to be there to see it. And he'd even lied to me about where he was going. I still couldn't understand that part. Why did he have to lie to me? Because he thought he was somehow betraying me by going rodeoing one more time when he'd promised to settle down here? Or could he have been scared— afraid that he really was finished as a bull rider? Maybe he just couldn't take the chance of having me there to see him try one more time—and fail. That would mean that what I thought mattered a lot more to him than I had ever realized. Still, any way you cut it, the whole thing made me feel left out, as if Dad hadn't trusted me to share the greatest ride he'd ever made. I didn't know whether to be proud or to get mad all over again.

Casey was waiting for me to say something, but I couldn't think of anything to say. Then Mrs. Sutherland came over, and I remembered I had to talk to her about something more important.

"Mrs. Sutherland?"

She closed the back doors of the van and turned around.

I didn't know exactly how I was going to say this, so I ended up blurting it out as fast as I could, the way I do oral reports in school. "Uh, I know we're going to owe you a bunch of money, and, well, I don't think we've got much, and since all this was my fault anyhow, I was wondering if you could maybe hold the bill till the holidays start, and I could find a job somewhere and get the money to pay you."

Her eyes were smiling, but she kept the rest of her face serious when she answered. "That sounds like a reasonable enough request." She looked me over hard then, like she would study a horse she might buy. Then she made up her mind. "But if you're really serious about a job, I've got one for you, starting Saturday morning at the clinic. Casey helps out Saturdays, but sometimes we get behind. You want it?"

"Sure," I said, trying not to sound as relieved as I felt.

"Okay, see you at nine on Saturday. Get in, Casey. I've got some chores to finish, and you've got homework."

Casey made a face. "I can't wait," she muttered as she climbed in. Her mother started the engine and was already turning around when Casey stuck her head out the window. "Hey, Shane, do you want to come to the school dance tomorrow night?"

That was the first I'd heard that there was one, but I didn't need to be asked twice. "Sure," I said again. Then I noticed Casey's face. She'd turned bright red and looked like she wished she could disappear. "I mean," she stammered, "Mom's taking Barb and me, and she'll stop for you, if you need a ride, that is."

That was the first time I'd seen Casey when she wasn't in control of the situation. I was kind of glad to see that I wasn't the only one who gets embarrassed. But I didn't really see what she had to be embarrassed about. I didn't mind going to the dance with her all that much.

I stood there and watched the van disappear up the hill. It wasn't until I heard a noise behind me and turned around to see Dad and Jeff standing there that I realized I still had a big, stupid grin on my face.

"Well, at least you ain't got bad taste," Jeff said, and then it was my turn to get embarrassed. I looked at Dad. He didn't say anything. He didn't seem to be mad at me anymore, but it was hard to tell because he avoided looking me in the eye. I didn't understand what he was thinking at all. I wasn't sure it wasn't better when I at least knew he was mad.

Then I remembered the newspaper article, and I had to ask. "Did you really score an eighty-eight at Cochrane, Dad?"

He did look at me when he answered. "Yeah, Shane, I really did. It was that ride I was always waitin' for." He stopped for a minute and then added, so low I almost didn't hear, "Too bad it had to come too late."

I started to say *What do you mean, too late? You can still be a champ,* but I didn't say it. Because, for once in his life, Dad was seeing things like they really were. He was thirty-six years old, he had a kid to be responsible for, a ranch he couldn't leave, a drinking problem he couldn't drown, and a memory he couldn't bury. He was right. It was too late. Not too late to be a great bull rider; he'd proved that. But too late to be a champ again. I can't explain it exactly, but they're two different things.

Then suddenly his face broke out in that thousand-watt grin of his that makes it hard to believe there's a stormy side to Josh Morgan. "But it was worth it," he said. "I'd almost forgot how it felt to walk up there and

pick up that first-prize money. And the silver buckle." He
pulled up his jacket so I could see it. It was a nice enough
buckle, all right. But he must have had a dozen more like
it . . . or better. Still, he seemed to be real proud of it,
so I walked over and took a good look.

"That's great, Dad. It's a real nice buckle." I sounded
as phony as a three-dollar bill, but I didn't know what to
do about it. I just didn't know what Dad expected from
me anymore. One minute he was acting like he wished I
didn't exist, and the next he was wanting my approval for
making a super ride. I didn't have a clue what part I was
supposed to be playing anymore.

But I hadn't seen anything yet. His next move was
enough to leave me wondering what movie I was in,
never mind which part.

"Oh, yeah," he said, with a kind of half-proud, half-
embarrassed expression. "I used some of that prize
money to buy you something." He hesitated there, not
seeming to know how I was going to react. Then he
started opening the doors of Jeff's horse trailer. "It's in
here," he said.

Of course, my first thought was that they really had
bought a horse in Cochrane, but that didn't make sense.
Irresponsible as those two could be about some things,
they'd never have left a horse standing in the trailer all
that time.

I was right. It wasn't a horse. It was a big, rugged
Yamaha YZ 100, all bright red and white, with its gold
rims shining in the sun.

I just stood there and didn't say a word. Maybe Dad
thought I was too happy for words. I hoped that's what
he thought. The truth is that I was stunned. All I could
hear was my brain ringing up numbers like a cash regis-

ter. At first glance I'd thought the bike was brand-new, but now I could see it had some miles on it. But even secondhand a bike like that must have cost him five or six hundred anyway. Some of the prize money! I'd have bet it was all the prize money and some more thrown in. I wondered if he'd been drunk when he bought it. I almost hoped so. The only alternative was that he was crazy.

He didn't have a job. He didn't have any prospects of getting a job, we were so close to broke I could almost hear the wolf scratching at the door, and he happened to pick up a little money he hadn't been counting on. So what did he do? Put it in the bank or buy groceries or something far-out like that? No. He went and bought me a motorcycle. I didn't even know if I wanted a motorcycle. The whole idea was so totally out of the question that I'd never even thought about it before.

One thing I did know for sure: If I had to pick between eating three meals a day and owning a motorcycle, eating would have won, hands down. But unfortunately Dad didn't seem to see it that way. He'd missed a few other little details, too, such as the fact that it wasn't legal for me to even ride a bike like this for another two years.

But none of that made any difference now, because, like it or not, I had the bike. It was sitting there in cold, hard metal, and I had to say something. But what? How about, *It's very nice, but I'm afraid you'll have to take it back?* That was what I wanted to say, but I knew I couldn't.

It was crazy. After the way Dad had acted last night when he'd seen Angel, I'd thought that he hated my guts. That nothing would ever make him forgive me for letting Mom's horse get hurt. Now something in his face gave me the weirdest feeling that suddenly he and I had switched places, and he was a kid, trying to win my ap-

proval any way he could. Was this his way of trying to say
he was sorry about all the times when I'd needed him and
he hadn't been there?

So why couldn't he just talk to me, tell me how he felt?
Did he think he could buy me a bike and that would wipe
out all the bad times? I didn't need a bike. I needed a
father. But I couldn't say that. I couldn't tell him how I
felt any better than he could tell me. So it looked like I
was going to have a bike.

I grinned a big, frozen grin and managed to say, "It's
beautiful, Dad. I just can't believe you really got it for
me." And I wasn't lying about that.

That broke the tension, and suddenly Dad and Jeff
were all over that machine, playing with it like kids with a
new toy. They got so carried away, they almost forgot all
about me, so I didn't have to keep up my excited look any
longer.

But I guess I'd have to admit that by the time I actually
got the chance to get on that bike and tear down the road
with the wind in my face and trees flashing past in a blur
and the chrome flashing in the sun and that big engine
roaring . . . loving that machine had stopped being
just an act. Whatever mixed-up reasons Dad had for
buying it, suddenly I was kind of glad he'd done it.

12

Friday wasn't very eventful at school, which was just as well, because I'd had about enough events for the week. Everybody seemed to be in a good mood, probably just because it was Friday. Even Mr. Thorpe stopped intersecting and gave us some nice, straightforward decimals.

When noon came, the last thing I felt like doing was running over that killer hill. There had to be more exciting ways to spend a lunch hour. Then I remembered that I'd already tried one of those ways, and I still had the bruises to prove it. Maybe running wasn't such a bad idea, after all.

I was standing by my locker trying to make up my mind about practice when Cheryl came along. "Hey, Shane, get changed. The coach will be waiting." I didn't say anything for a minute. "You are coming, aren't you? We really need you." She stood there, smiling at me.

"Yeah, sure I'm coming," I said. Running that hill was hard, but it wasn't as hard as trying to tell Cheryl I wouldn't run it.

I went to the washroom and put on my shorts. Well,

actually they were an old pair of jeans I'd ripped the knee out of riding steers, so I'd chopped them off. The left leg was about an inch longer than the right, and they'd frayed out into long fringes, but I didn't think that would bother my running any. I didn't think the coach would like them much, but that was his problem. I didn't have the money or the desire to own a pair of those cute little red ones the school store sold.

I met a couple of the other guys getting changed, and we wandered out to the hill together. It was a hot day for June, and given half a chance, I would have sprawled out in the sun like a big lazy cat and had a nice nap.

I wasn't given half a chance. There was the coach, all hot to trot in his blue and white sweat suit. I guess he always wore it, whatever the weather was like, but he never did anything to work up a sweat in it.

"Okay, everybody gather round. Let's get this show on the road!" He glanced around, checking to see if he had everybody. Then the coach's eyes swept over me, stopped, came back, and settled on me. He was going to complain about my shorts, I could tell. I stared back at him, waiting, half-hoping for him to kick me off his cross-country team. We looked at each other for a few long seconds. Then, without a word to me, he turned away and went on giving instructions. I knew then that, A: he didn't like me. And, B: he was going to put up with me anyway.

He had the stopwatch in his hand. "Go!" he yelled as he clicked the button. We all sprinted the hundred yards of level ground, but as we started up that sun-baked hillside I dropped into a slow jog. I wasn't about to get carried away with this stuff. Besides, I didn't want to have to go fight with the cockroaches, or whatever those little critters were in the shower room. Maybe if I was careful, I wouldn't work up a sweat.

Then a familiar voice behind me called, "Shane! You did come!" And there was Cheryl, moving up beside me, smiling.

"Yeah," I said and smiled back.

She moved ahead a couple of paces and looked back at me. "Come on, let's get out of the dust." I caught up to her. We didn't seem to be running very fast, but the next thing I knew, we'd passed everyone except Jim Nelson, who was already out of sight. I was getting tired, so I slowed down a little. Cheryl pulled ahead a few steps. She looked over her shoulder. "Hey, Shane, what are you waiting for? Getting tired?" she asked. She wasn't even puffing.

"No!" I said and speeded up.

Don't ask me which is worse, running to beat a guy you hate, or to impress a girl you like.

I took five seconds off yesterday's time. The coach was happy. Cheryl was happy. But I was mad. After a run like that I'd have to take a shower, after all.

As we headed for the school Cheryl called, "See you at the dance tonight, Shane." She was hardly even breathing hard.

"Sure!" I gasped, trying to pretend I was hardly even breathing hard.

As the bus started down into our valley I leaned over and looked out at our yard. Alvin had the window pretty well jelly-fingerprinted, but I could still see what I wanted to see.

It was there, in the driveway. The big, red, mean machine. Last night seemed so long ago that I'd started wondering if I might have dreamed it up. Things would have been simpler if I had dreamed it. But if I had to have one more problem, I could have done worse than that bike.

Suddenly Alvin spotted it. "Hey, is that your motorcycle, Shane?" he asked, all big eyes and missing teeth.

"Yeah."

"Where'd you get it?"

"From my dad."

"Was it your birthday?"

"Nope."

"Then why'd he get it for you?"

Now there was a smart question, even coming from Alvin. "Oh, for being good, I guess," I said as I got off. It was as good an answer as any.

I dumped my books on the back step and polished a little dust off the bike with my shirttail. The bike still seemed kind of unreal, like it might turn into a pumpkin at midnight or something, but that didn't stop me from thinking I'd just take it out for a little ride, right now. I climbed on, a second too late. Jeff's voice stopped me. "Oh, no, you don't, Short Stuff. We are workin', and you are helpin', so just crawl off that machine and get yourself over here."

He and Dad were rebuilding a piece of corral that was about to fall down. It was obvious that neither of those big-time cowboys counted corral-building very high on their list of things to do. They sure seemed glad to see me. You know what they say about misery loving company.

An hour later I had four thousand slivers and a purple thumbnail. But we had the fence fixed.

Dad cooked supper this time. And compared to Jeff, Dad is an expert. His hamburgers tasted almost like real food. I ate five.

Mrs. Sutherland was picking me up at seven, so I had to hurry and get cleaned up. It wasn't easy with Dad and Jeff watching every move and Jeff making helpful remarks. Dad was still being kind of quiet. Maybe I would have tried to get him to talk if I hadn't been in such a hurry. He might even have been interested in the fact that I'd made the cross-country team. I wondered if he'd have been a little bit proud. But I didn't have time to find out.

I couldn't decide if I wanted to wear a T-shirt or a cowboy shirt. Most of the guys would probably wear T-shirts, but I didn't have one that was in real good health. Anyhow, I wasn't most of the guys. I wore the green and white cowboy shirt Dad had given me for Christmas. I'd had to throw my respectable blue jeans into the washer just before supper, and they were still a little damp when I put them on. It's not the most comfortable feeling, but it's guaranteed to get them pressed into shape without touching an iron.

It was five to seven when I started out the door to meet Mrs. Sutherland at the road. I was just saying good-bye when Jeff interrupted. "Josh, your kid is beginnin' to look like the last of the big-time hippies. He needs a haircut."

Dad looked kind of surprised, like he hadn't really noticed he had me for the last few years. "Yeah," he agreed. "He is gettin' kind of hard to find, ain't he?"

"Yup. And I saw some scissors in one of these drawers.
. . ."

I finally found a good use for all that cross-country
practice. I was out at the road before he could remember
which drawer.

13

Casey and her friend, Barb, were already in the back seat, so I sat in the front with Casey's mom. It was kind of funny how Casey was acting half-spooked around me ever since she'd invited me to go to the dance with them. I guess she was afraid I'd think she was chasing me. She didn't need to worry; I didn't think that.

And even if it had been true, I wouldn't have considered it a fate worse than death.

The dance had just started when we pulled into the parking lot. The car windows were open, and the sound of AC/DC drifted in.

"Are you going to stay for the dance, Mrs. Sutherland?" Barb asked.

Mrs. Sutherland shuddered. "Not on your life, Barb. I chaperoned one of these things once. I think it caused permanent hearing impairment."

"Oh, Mom," Casey said. "The music isn't that loud."

"What'd you say, Case?"

"I said, 'It's not that loud.' "

"Eh?"

"It's not that—" Casey yelled. Then she started to laugh, and we all broke up. Her mom was one crazy lady. Maybe that's why I liked her so much.

"I'll pick you up at ten," she said as we got out. "Be good and have fun—in that order!"

As soon as we got in the school, Casey and Barb disappeared into the bathroom with about three quarters of the female population. From the amount of time all the girls spent in there, you'd think they didn't have indoor plumbing at home.

I'd never got around to going to a dance at any of the other schools, so I leaned against the wall and tried to be inconspicuous while I figured out what was happening. The answer to that question turned out to be simple. Nothing. Even though it was still broad daylight outside, it was dark in the gym, except for the disc jockey's flashing lights. He did have a pretty good light show, and his sound system was really belting out the sound. But nobody was dancing. The girls were either still holding court in the can or giggling in little bunches on the east side of the gym. The guys were either walking back and forth to the Coke machine or swapping lies in little bunches on the west side of the gym.

I spotted Greg and Pete and a couple of other guys I knew sitting on the benches against the wall, so I wandered over and sat down with them. We went and got Cokes and then came back and sat listening to the music and looking at the girls. Except that it was really hard to see them away over there. There were a few parent chaperones walking around with pained expressions, looking like they wished they'd brought their aspirins.

Then Miss Bradley strolled through. She seemed to be sort of running things, and she kept trying to convince somebody to start dancing, since every minute of music (she kind of hesitated over the word *music*) was costing the Students' Union money. She even threatened that if we didn't soon ask some girls to dance, we'd have to take turns dancing with her. I think she was bluffing, but we all headed for the bathroom, just in case.

All the wandering around went on for about half an hour. Then the DJ put on one of those songs with a real loud beat that everybody likes to stomp to, and a few of the "in" kids got up and started to dance. That was all it took. Everybody started dancing.

Well, not quite everybody. I think there must be a few kids who go just to watch everybody else. It's not a bad idea. I was sitting there, figuring out the whole social structure of Deer Valley Junior High in one easy lesson, when I felt a hand on my shoulder. I turned, and there was Cheryl. "Hi, Shane. Aren't you going to ask me to dance?"

Well, that was a unique approach. I wondered what would have happened if I'd said no. But I didn't say it. She really was a good-looking girl.

I hadn't danced all that much before, and I didn't have a clue what I was doing, but looking around, I was pretty sure hardly anybody else did either.

A lot of people took a second look at us, and since not that many people knew me, I guessed it was Cheryl they were looking at. I was beginning to realize that she was one of the most popular girls in the school. Why she was bothering with me, I didn't know, but I didn't waste my energy worrying about it.

The song ended, and we went and sat down. She was just going to say something when somebody asked her to dance. She looked a little bit mad, but she went. I looked around and saw that Casey and Barb had finally come out. Casey was looking in my direction, so I grinned and went and asked her to dance. She wasn't as good a dancer as Cheryl, not as sure of herself. But I kind of liked that about her.

The song ended, and we went back to where she'd been sitting. Barb was still there, looking kind of lonely. She was a real quiet girl, and I didn't know her very well, but I liked her. And I knew she wasn't Casey's best friend for nothing. So I asked her to dance. Casey flashed me a thank-you look that would have made dancing with Dracula seem worthwhile.

Casey was dancing with Greg by the end of the song, and when I took Barb back, Pete asked her to dance. I went and sat down by the door. It was getting awful hot in there.

Cheryl was dancing with someone a lot taller than her. Then the light flashed across his face, and I saw that it was Bart Willard. That sort of surprised me, but not as much as it might have. In his own way Bart was a guy everybody noticed. And Cheryl was the sort of girl who managed to get noticed, too. They danced about three dances in a row together. Cheryl saw me sitting there by the door as they went past and flashed me a big smile a couple of times.

The next time the music stopped, a lot of people sat down. But I noticed that Cheryl and Bart were still out there. It looked like they were arguing about something. Suddenly she shook his hand off her arm and walked off, leaving him standing in the middle of the floor. She came straight over to me.

"Shane, dance with me, please," she said, really upset, almost like she was going to cry. I glanced across the gym, and even in the dim light I could feel Bart's eyes burning into me. Danger signals were going off like rockets in my brain.

"Please, Shane," she repeated, looking at me with those big, brown eyes. I danced with her.

At the end of the song I started to take her back to the bench, but she didn't move. So, rather than drag her off the floor, I danced with her again. And again. I was getting embarrassed. A lot of people were staring at us, and I was beginning to get the feeling that everyone but me understood what was happening. I wouldn't have cared, except that I seemed to be one of the main participants. And one of the people staring was Casey.

After the third dance Cheryl was finally ready to sit down. We walked over to the benches, and she sat down right beside the open door. I thought maybe I could leave her there and take a walk to the bathroom or something, but she was holding on to my hand, so sitting down beside her was the most inconspicuous thing I could think of to do.

She shivered. "Oh, am I ever cold!" she said and snuggled up real close to me. If looks could kill, the one Casey gave me then would have been fatal, even across the gym.

I stood up and pulled Cheryl up, too. "Come on," I said.

"Where are we going?"

"To get you warmed up," I said. She looked at me under her eyelashes and came along.

I remembered from phys. ed. class that afternoon that there was one heat register in that gym that never shut off, even if it was 90 above in there. Sure enough, it was still blowing hot air. It felt like an oven next to the register.

"Sit down," I said to Cheryl.

She was too confused to argue. She sat, and I pulled my hand loose. "You'll soon get warmed up here," I said and walked out of the gym.

The dance lasted another hour, but it was over right then as far as I was concerned. I got a Coke and went and sat by myself in a corner of the gym. The music was giving me a headache. If anybody'd asked me right then, I'd even have admitted that when it came right down to it, I liked Kenny Rogers better than AC/DC anyhow. That stupid strobe light was making me dizzy. And I had just decided that I still liked horses better than girls. Well, better than most girls. . . .

At a quarter to ten I decided to go out and wait for Mrs. Sutherland in the parking lot. I was just going through the front doors when Greg stopped me. "I wouldn't go out there, Shane."

"Why not?"

"Bart Willard's waiting for you, and it's not for a visit. He's mad."

I just about said "What about?" but the pieces were all falling into place, and I already knew the answer. I also knew that whatever Cheryl had been trying to prove to Bart, she had set me up, real good. Sometimes I couldn't believe the messes I could get myself into.

I looked out the window. Bart was there, all right. Leaning on a car, waiting.

Well, I might as well get it over with. I took a deep breath and started to open the door. A hand on my shoulder stopped me. I looked around. It was Miss Bradley, and I had a pretty good idea that she knew exactly what was going on.

"I can forbid you to go out that door, Shane." She stood there, her eyes searching my face, wondering if I understood what she was trying to tell me.

I understood. She was giving me the perfect out if I needed it. Nobody can call you chicken if the teacher stops you.

I met her look. "And are you going to forbid me to go out?" I asked.

"I think I'll leave that up to you."

I thought about that for a minute and realized what she was giving me. Something you don't get too often from adults. Trust. And a chance to make my own choice. I knew which choice I had to make if I was going to be able to live with myself.

"It's not the only way," I said.

She nodded. "Okay, Shane. Handle it your own way." She started to walk away.

Then I remembered something. "Miss Bradley?" She stopped and looked back at me. "Thanks," I said. She smiled and walked into the staff room.

Bart watched me come out of the school. "You looking for me?" I asked.

"Yeah."

"Why?"

"Don't play games with me, Morgan. You know why. Cheryl's going with me. And if you think you're big enough to change that, maybe you better prove it to me, right now."

I looked at him, and he was just as big, and just as tough, and he could probably lick me again, just as bad, but I was too tired of this whole business to care much.

"Bart," I said, "there's two things I want you to know. One, I didn't know Cheryl was your girl friend. It doesn't show a whole lot, the way she acts. And two, I'm probably not big enough to take her away from you. But that's something you'll never find out. Because I don't want her."

Bart didn't say anything. We just stood there staring at each other for a few seconds. Then I turned and walked away. He didn't follow.

14

I didn't wake up in the greatest mood Saturday morning, and I was just ready to roll over and go back to sleep when it occurred to me that I had to be at work by nine. I crawled out of bed.

There was a lot of crashing and banging going on in the kitchen, so I went to check it out. Dad and Jeff were getting breakfast. That is, Dad was getting breakfast. Jeff was making coffee and noise. Breakfast was good. The coffee was bad.

I helped clean up the dishes and then grabbed my jacket and started for the door. "Where you headed, Shane?" Dad asked, and I realized that I'd never mentioned having this job.

"Oh, I forgot to tell you. I'm working for Mrs. Sutherland for a while. Till I get the vet bill for Angel paid off, anyhow." I tried to make it sound like it was no big deal, but I didn't know how he'd feel about it.

After the way he'd acted after Angel got cut, I felt like he might blow sky-high again anytime the subject came up. What he'd said that night had tore me up so bad that

I could still feel the knife edge of his voice cut into me when he'd said, "I should've known better than to trust you with *her* horse." I'd always known Dad had a quick temper, and I'd seen him mad at me a lot of times, but I'd never known him to fight that dirty before. There was no way I was ready to handle another guilt trip like he'd laid on me that night.

I just stood there, trying to act cool and unconcerned, but inside I was so tense I felt like I could explode. He gave me a funny look, and at first I was afraid he was mad again. But his voice didn't sound mad, just kind of sad. "You don't have to do that, Shane," he said, real quiet.

"Yeah, I do." I hoped he'd understand. And for once I think he did.

He looked at me for a long time, as if he was trying to find the right words to say what was on his mind. Finally he just nodded and said, "Okay, if it's what you want." He walked on outside, but as he went by he put his arm around my shoulders and gave me kind of an awkward squeeze. That was the closest thing to a hug I'd had from him for a long time. It made me wonder about a lot of things. About how hard it seemed to be for him to let any of his feelings out. But mostly I wondered if he had felt as bad about saying those words as I had felt about hearing them. Maybe what he'd just done was about as close as a Morgan could come to saying he was sorry.

I was ready to get on the bike and ride up to the Sutherlands' when two things changed my mind. One was a sneaking suspicion that somebody who worked with animals all the time, and who did everything as quiet as Mrs. Sutherland did, might just hate motorcycles. And the last thing I wanted was to get her mad at me, too. It had been an awful quiet ride home last night, and I could tell that Casey was none too happy.

The other reason was that good old Reb was standing there looking over the fence at me, whinnying and generally acting like a neglected child. So I gave in.

I rode into the Sutherlands' yard and tied Reb up in the shade. That was one classy layout. It looked even bigger and fancier close up. I rang the office doorbell, and Mrs. Sutherland came out, munching on a piece of toast.

"Morning, Shane. As you can see, we're a little slow this morning. Come in while I get organized." I followed her a few miles through the house to a big, comfortable kitchen, where Casey and a man were eating breakfast.

"Roger," Mrs. Sutherland said, "this is our new neighbor, Shane Morgan. Shane, this is my husband."

He stood up and shook hands with me. "Nice to meet you, Shane."

I tried not to stare at him, but it wasn't easy. Not that there was anything strange about him. He was about the most ordinary man I'd ever seen, kind of small with graying hair, a neat gray moustache, and serious gray eyes. Even though he was wearing blue jeans and a faded shirt, I felt like he should have had on a neat gray suit.

But the thing that surprised me about him was that he existed at all. I realize that there are a few kids with two parents left in the world, but in the time I'd known Casey, a grand total of four days, she'd never mentioned her father. And her mother was always so much in control of the situation that I'd just assumed she and Casey were on their own.

"Roger's a lawyer and has his office in Calgary, so we don't see much of each other during the week. We try to find time to at least visit a little on Saturdays. That's why we are going shopping and you kids are cleaning the clinic." She automatically poured me a glass of milk and passed the toast. I'd eaten half an hour ago, but I tried not to let that stand in my way.

"Okay, time to get to work," she said a few minutes later, when she'd drained her third cup of coffee. "I'll be ready to go to town in about half an hour, Rog. Casey, aren't you coming to help show Shane around?"

"I'll be there in a few minutes. I have to clean my room." Those were the first words Casey had said since I walked in the door.

Her mother shrugged. "Now, that is a first. Heaven knows what's got into her this time."

Heaven might know, but I had a strong suspicion.

The clinic was right behind the office, and Mrs. Sutherland gave me the complete guided tour. She got so wrapped up in telling me about what everything was for and why each animal was there that I began to wonder if she'd really get around to her shopping trip at all. She loved that placed so much, I don't think she'd have cared much if she never got around to it, but her husband looked like the type who liked things to run on schedule.

After she showed me how to clean the cages in the small-animal section, she took me through a covered walkway to a super-clean little barn where she had a couple of calves and a horse she was treating. "This is the really educational part of the job," she said. "Ph D level, in fact. You just take this fork, clean out the stall, carry it out to the wagon, and pile it on, higher and deeper!" She laughed and checked her watch. "Okay, got to get going. Casey'll help you if she ever gets done whatever she thinks she's doing. The two of you should finish around noon. But you're welcome to stay and visit as long as you like. We'll be back sometime this afternoon."

Casey took her sweet time in coming out. I was almost finished cleaning up when she finally came out and started changing the drinking water in the cages. She didn't even look in my direction, so I gave up pretending it was all in my imagination. She really wasn't talking to me. Well, standing there holding a pan of kitty litter might not be the best position for a heart-to-heart talk, but I'd had enough of the silent treatment.

"Okay, Case, why don't you say it?"

She didn't look at me. "Say what?"

"Whatever it is that's on your mind."

"I don't know what you're talking about." She kept on walking and went on with what she was doing, as if I didn't exist. When she finished, she walked out the back door. She didn't exactly slam it. Just shut it kind of hard.

It took me another fifteen minutes to finish my share of the work. I spent that time getting good and mad. Maybe she did have a right to be jealous, but I had just as much right to tell my side of the story.

I closed the door kind of hard, too, and walked outside, looking for her. She was nowhere in sight. I was just ready to give up and climb on Reb and go home when he cocked his ears to the west and whinnied. Casey was about a quarter of a mile away, just disappearing over the top of a hill, riding her blue roan horse.

The sensible thing to do would still have been to go home. But since when have us Morgans been famous for being sensible? Besides, I had a few things I really wanted to say to her. And she didn't have that much of a head start.

Reb had spent a boring morning. When I hit the saddle, he started to run. I pointed him in the direction Casey had gone, and he burned up that trail just like the YZ would have. Only quieter. We were only about a hundred yards behind them when both Casey and the roan took a surprised look over their shoulders. That horse leaped ahead like he'd sat on a wasp, and Casey didn't try to discourage him. It was going to be a race if I wanted to catch her, and old Reb had just enough Thoroughbred in him to love the idea. We gained another fifty yards before Blue hit his stride, and then the distance between us stayed the same. It was beginning to look like it would come down to whichever one of us was willing to run our horse until he dropped. And after almost doing that to Reb once I knew I'd never do it again.

I was starting to rein him in when I saw the gleam of a big sheet of water, straight ahead. The trail we were on was one that cattle used to go to drink out of a big beaver dam in the creek, and it came to a dead end right at the water's edge. I turned Reb off the trail at an angle to cut Casey off from turning downstream, and her horse slid to a stop beside the dam. That water was deep.

"You've got two choices, Case!" I yelled. "Talk to me or take a swim."

She gave me a dirty glare. "Don't tempt me," she muttered. Blue snorted and pawed the ground impatiently. "Oh, stop it, you stupid horse!" she snapped at him and jumped off, dropping the reins and leaving him ground-tied there as she stalked over to the edge of the dam, flung herself down, and started viciously beheading dandelions and throwing them in the water.

I walked over and sat down beside her. She didn't look at me.

"Listen, Casey, if it's about last night . . ."

Rip! There went another dandelion. I had an uneasy feeling that she wished it was my head instead.

"I didn't mean it to happen that way. I mean Cheryl and me . . . I couldn't help it."

That got Casey's attention. "You couldn't help it! Oh, that's beautiful, Shane! Poor, helpless Shane Morgan kidnapped by the deadly and dangerous Cheryl Anderson!"

"Come on, Casey. Quit it! You know what I mean. Look, she came over to me, practically crying, and asked me to dance with her. What was I supposed to do? Slug her?"

Casey shook her head. "Shane, you are so gullible."

Gullible? Now there was another of those ten-dollar words. But I supposed if Casey said I was gullible, I probably was gullible. And she wasn't finished with me yet.

"Cheryl's got to collect every trophy there is. And I don't mean just for running. And last night she was going for double or nothing. Playing you and Bart against each other. But I suppose you never noticed that."

"Yeah, I noticed all right. But by then it was a little late. By that time you weren't talking to me, and Bart was waiting to fight me."

Casey's eyes widened. "You fought Bart again?"

"I'm not bleeding, am I? No, I didn't fight him. I told him I wouldn't want Cheryl if she was the last girl on earth."

Casey had stopped murdering dandelions and was staring straight ahead, but she was smiling a little. Just enough to make her dimples show. "You really told Bart that?"

"Yeah, and Casey . . ." I reached over and gently

turned her face around so I could see it. "It's the truth, believe me."

We looked at each other for a long time. Then she really did smile. "I believe you. You're just dumb enough for it to be true." Then she got kind of red. "I guess I wouldn't have minded so much if I hadn't practically dragged you to that dance in the first place. I felt pretty stupid."

"Welcome to the club."

"So how'd Bart react when you told him that about Cheryl?"

"It was pretty strange. He didn't do anything. I expected to get my face punched in. And you weren't even there to rescue me this time."

"It really bothers you that I did that, doesn't it?"

I shrugged. "Well, it didn't bother me that he quit beating on me. But it's not the greatest thing for a guy's pride when a girl bails him out of a fight he's losing. And one thing I never did get . . . why'd Bart listen to you, anyhow?"

"There are a lot of things you don't know about Bart. You think he's just a big, stupid hood who has to solve everything by beating somebody up. And he is. But a lot of things have happened to make him like that. Ever since his parents split up, way back when he was in kindergarten, they've been trading him back and forth like an extra piece of furniture. Bart just couldn't handle living like that, and he's been getting into all sorts of trouble ever since. Once, when he was really having a rough time, he stayed with us for nearly a year. Mom's a real stray collector, animal and human. So I guess Bart's never forgotten that he was almost like a brother to me once. He still treats me kind of special, and in spite of everything, I can't help liking him a little, too. So try not to hold the way he is against him too much. He can't help it."

"I don't know, Case. A person can't go on forever using something bad that's happened to them for an excuse. Sometime you've got to learn to live with it." At first I thought I was talking about Bart, but then, way back in my mind, I wondered if maybe I was thinking about somebody else. Dad? Or even myself? Deep down I had a sneaking suspicion that both Dad and I could have used that piece of advice.

Casey threw one more dandelion to a watery death. "You expect too much from people sometimes, Shane."

I threw her a quick glance. "What's that supposed to mean?" She looked back at me with those steady gray eyes, and I got the uneasy feeling that in some ways she understood me better than I did myself. Maybe some of the things I hadn't told her about Dad and me showed up pretty well without telling. "You know what it means," she said.

I was afraid if we kept talking long enough, we'd manage to work our way around to a brand-new fight. I glanced over to where the horses were grazing and found a way to change the subject. Casey had one of those fancy wool saddle blankets with her initials worked into it. "I thought you spelled your name with a *C*. How come it says *KCS* on there?"

She gave me a mysterious look. "Cross your heart and hope to die and I'll tell you a deep, dark secret."

I did.

"My real name is Katrina Constance Sutherland. Pretty heavy, huh? My dad's idea. Old family names and stuff. He's a real traditional kind of person. But Mom took pity on me and started calling me by my initials and, thank heaven, it stuck." She stood up. "Are you coming riding with me, or are you going to sit here asking dumb questions all day?"

15

Jeff went home on Sunday. I don't know why it should have come as any big surprise to me. He had a wife and two little kids waiting for him back in Cheyenne, and I knew that after being gone for more than a week he was missing them a lot. I didn't blame him for wanting to get back home. But until he started packing, I hadn't realized how big a space he was filling between Dad and me.

While Dad was getting breakfast I helped Jeff carry some of his stuff out to his truck. I didn't think the way I was feeling was so obvious, but as I turned back toward the house he stopped me. "Hey, Short Stuff, hold on a minute." I turned, and Jeff pushed back his hat and leaned against the fender. "I don't want to drive out of here with you lookin' like you just lost your last friend."

I bent over and jerked a thread off the bottom of my jeans so he couldn't see my face when I answered. "Then you better not drive out of here, 'cause when you do, I will have."

"Aw, come on, Shane. You know better than that. I can't stay forever, and you and Josh are gonna have to

figure things out between you someday, ain't you?" I
knew the answer he expected to hear, so I nodded miser-
ably.

"Yeah, I guess."

"And do you think it's gonna get any easier in another
week? Or a month? Or a year?"

I shook my head.

"That's right. It ain't never gonna be easy. But it can
be done. If you and Josh try hard enough. And I'll tell
you this, kid: Josh has made his mistakes, and he ain't
always been the world's champion father. He'd be the
first one to admit it. But he really is tryin' now. The next
move's up to you. Give him a chance and try not to
expect more than he can give."

I didn't say anything. That last line sounded familiar. It
seemed like everybody had been practicing the same
lecture lately.

Jeff reached his long arm over and messed up my hair.
"You'll be okay. Just don't forget what I told you before.
Sometimes you can't fight your way out. You just gotta
keep untangling things, slow and easy."

Monday morning Dad was up and had breakfast ready by
the time I woke up. Still, the house seemed awful quiet
with just the two of us there.

I got dressed and went out to the kitchen, but Dad was
already finished eating. I wondered what the hurry was.
He dished me up some eggs and cleared off his own
dishes.

I started getting suspicious. Finally I asked, "You going somewhere?"

"Yeah, I'm goin' to work." I shouldn't have looked so

surprised. It was just that I couldn't remember Dad ever going to work in the morning, like most people do.

"Well, if we're plannin' on eatin' much longer, we're gonna need some money." I couldn't argue with that.

"What are you going to work at?"

"Drivin' a grader for the county. Saw the job advertised in the paper, so I went and talked to the foreman."

"You don't know how to drive a grader." I didn't mean it as if he was stupid or something, but I didn't think he'd ever done anything but rodeo.

"Sure I do. Worked at it down in Montana for a couple of years when you were just a baby. Before I started makin' enough money ridin' bulls."

It was time for both of us to go. He put on his beat-up old hat and waved and grinned as he drove off. But I knew it was all a show. He hated machinery of any kind, and grinding along in the dust on a grader was going to drive him snaky.

I couldn't stop thinking about it all the time I was waiting for the bus. Josh Morgan, two-time world champion bull rider, riding a road grader. Jeff must have known about it. No wonder he'd said that Dad was really trying hard. But I had almost liked it better when Dad was sneaking off to rodeos. At least then I could be mad at him. But I knew there was only one thing that would ever make him tie himself to a job like grader driving. Me. Me and this crazy, strings-attached ranch. It made me feel guilty. And guilty is a lot worse than mad.

I was depressed even before I got on the bus and discovered that Alvin had brought a gallon jar full of ants for show and tell . . . and he'd just dropped and broken the jar under our seat.

Amazingly enough, it turned out to be not too bad a

week at school. Nobody was more surprised than I was that I kept turning up for cross-country practice. I still hated it, but I was starting to get just a little curious about how much I could cut my time if I really worked on it. I had to do it on my own, though. Cheryl didn't run with me anymore.

The Zone Championships tryouts were after school on Thursday. I told the coach I couldn't stay because Dad was working and I didn't have a ride home. He said I was going to run even if he had to drive me home himself.

I ran. I placed fourth, behind Jim Nelson, a guy from another school, and good old Bart. I'd really thought I could beat him again, but he was just a little too far ahead when I made my move. Or maybe I just wasn't quite mad enough at him anymore.

But fourth in Zones wasn't bad. It meant I was on the team for Provincials in Edmonton. It also meant that I got to keep practicing for more than another week. As the guy once said about his own execution, "If it wasn't for the honor, I don't think I'd bother to show up."

Dad seemed to be hanging in pretty good with the job. As far as I knew, he hadn't had a drink since the Cochrane Rodeo and he was even starting to talk about getting enough money to buy some cows.

A few times I caught myself thinking that maybe we were going to get a nice little ranch going and live happily ever after here. But I always stopped myself. You don't erase four years overnight. Still, maybe if I just didn't expect too much, too soon . . .

Mrs. Sutherland checked Angel that weekend and said that she was doing great and might as well be out with the other horses, as long as we kept salve on the cut to keep the flies off.

I'd personally torn out every foot of that old wire fence, but I still couldn't help feeling goose pimples climb my spine when Dad opened the corral gate and she tore out of there at a kind of lopsided gallop. She was flying that white tail just as proud as ever, and it seemed like a replay of that other time. Maybe Angel was going to be a cripple, but nobody had thought to tell her. She still thought she was a princess.

Then I caught a glimpse of Dad's face as he stood there watching her, and the sunshine went out of the day. Maybe the horse wasn't hurting anymore, but he was. I think that taking special care of Angel was the one thing he'd felt he could still do for Mom. And thanks to me he hadn't even been able to do that. I wondered if he'd ever really deep-down forgive me for that. I wondered if I would.

School got really busy the next week. It was getting close to the end of the year, and we were reviewing for finals. I was still doing okay in most of my classes, but I'd found out that there was a lot of stuff I'd missed somewhere along the line, so for the first time in my life I was actually doing homework. Maybe that's why it didn't register that Dad was getting quieter and quieter. Even though he came home bone-tired and aching from sitting on that grader all day, he went out right after supper every night and worked on the fences until dark. And in June in Alberta dark comes pretty late. When he did come in, he wouldn't say much, just sit there reading old copies of *The Rodeo News.* I know that I should have been able to read the signs, but with Provincials coming up on Saturday and exams the next week, I just had too much else on my mind.

Then on Thursday, when I came home from school, there was a strange truck and camper sitting in the yard. When I walked up the lane, I found two big Stetsons lying on the grass, and under them were two big bull riders. Jake Cassidy and Bob Delvin. Next to Jeff they were about the best friends Dad had.

They heard me coming and sat up. "Hey, is this really Josh's kid? I was thinkin' he was still about eight years old."

"Yeah, it's him, all right. Looks a whole lot like his mama did, don't he, Bob?"

"Yup. He does at that." I was starting to get embarrassed by the time they finally stopped talking about me and started talking to me. Jake slapped me on the back. "Good to see you again, Shane. Real nice little place you fellas have got here. But where's your old man hiding out? We got some celebratin' to do. He tells us he's comin' up here to settle down, and the next thing you know, he's picked himself up a little eighty-eight point ride!"

I told him about Dad's job.

Bob looked at me like he thought I was making it all up. Then he looked at Jake. "Josh Morgan is driving a grader," he said slowly.

It was like I'd just told him a Kentucky Derby winner was pulling a beer wagon. I changed the subject. "What are you guys doing way up here?"

Jake shook his head and grinned. "You really are out of touch, way out here in the sticks. There's a big rodeo in Red Deer this weekend, so we just came up a day early to see old Josh and maybe pick up a free meal or two."

That reminded me it was nearly suppertime. Cowboys are usually pretty big eaters, so I really outdid myself. I cooked up three boxes of Kraft Dinner.

I never did decide if Dad was happy or sad to see Jake and Bob. Of course, he acted real happy, but I happened to see his face once when he didn't think anyone was looking, and there was something haunted about it.

We showed them around the place after supper, and then, about dark, we all headed inside. Jake made a detour to the camper and came back carrying a paper bag. "Got some glasses, Josh? It's time we drank to your big ride." He uncorked a bottle of whiskey and started pouring.

I went cold inside. *No!* I wanted to scream. *Don't do it, Dad! Don't throw it all away!* But, of course, I didn't say that. I didn't say anything. I just stood there in the kitchen, leaning on the fridge, watching as if it was all happening on TV. I could see everything that was going on, but I wasn't part of the scene.

Jake held out a glass. "Drink up, Josh. It's your party."

For the longest moment of my life Dad hesitated. He wanted to say no. I could almost feel him thinking it. Then it was as if there was a magnet in that glass and Dad's hand was made of steel. Slowly, shaking ever so slightly, that hand reached out.

He raised the glass, and as he did his eyes met mine. For the first time I could remember, Dad's eyes were the first to waver. He looked back at his friends and drained the glass. Jake poured another. "Hey, Shane. Didn't mean to forget you. There's some Coke here." He started to get me a glass, but I shook my head. "I've got homework," I muttered.

I went into my room and shut the door. Then I sat for

two hours with my science book open in front of me without turning a page. I couldn't concentrate. Even through the closed door I could hear the voices in the kitchen getting louder. And Dad's was the loudest and the drunkest of them all.

Over and over I kept thinking it. *He hasn't changed. Things are never going to be any different.*

16

The morning sun was bright enough to wake me up even though I hadn't had much sleep, so I walked into the kitchen about the usual time. A couple of empty bottles and three glasses were on the table. I dumped them in the sink and grabbed a glass of milk. All I wanted was to get out of there as fast as I could.

I was standing facing the window when I heard footsteps behind me. I turned and saw Dad, shaved and dressed—and looking like Death itself. He didn't say anything, just dumped a lot of instant coffee in his cup and poured the hot water in. His hand was shaking so bad he almost scalded himself. He gulped down the coffee and grabbed his hat. He had driven away by the time I went outside. There was no sign of life around the camper.

I thought about Dad all the way to school. He hadn't licked the drinking, after all. That was for sure. But what really surprised me was that, hangover and all, he cared enough about keeping that job to get up in the morning and go to work. You win some, you lose some, I guess.

Then I got to school, and I was too busy to think about him anymore. First thing, in language arts, we had to do oral book reports. Well, the book part's easy enough. I'd read about twenty of them so far this year. But talking in front of the class is something else. I get really nervous.

I had decided to do my report on *The Outsiders* by S. E. Hinton. I've read it about five times, and I never get tired of it. I guess it's because I can understand how those kids felt about being on the outside, looking in. I've been there, too.

After we were all finished, Miss Bradley called us up, one at a time, and told us our marks and why we got them.

"Shane," she said, "your report showed a lot of sensitivity and the ability to identify with the characters. You made me really want to read that book. However"—*however* should be officially rated as a dirty word; nothing good ever follows—"however, your style of presentation left something to be desired. . . ." The bell rang for break just then, and she dismissed the rest of the class. "Stick around a minute, Shane. I'm not quite through with you," she said in that semitough style that usually means she likes you. I grinned and waited by her desk.

"Now, as I was saying, about your speaking style . . . Well, to put it bluntly, you remind me of a horse in nose-fly season. You tossed your head so many times to get your hair out of your eyes that I was ready to get you a tie-down. However"—she fished around in her messy desk and brought out something in her hand—"if you don't get a haircut by next week, I will solve your problem with this." She opened her hand and dangled six inches of pink satin ribbon in front of my eyes. She raised one eyebrow. "Have I made myself perfectly clear?"

"Clear enough," I said. She was bluffing . . . probably. But since the stores were open late that night, I might just get Dad to bring me in for a haircut, just to humor her.

The truck and camper were gone from the yard when I got home, so I guessed that Jake and Bob had gone on to Red Deer. Too bad they'd had to stop here just long enough to mess up our world. It was funny. I liked those guys. They'd always been good to me, and I knew they'd do most anything for Dad. But they didn't come anywhere close to understanding him. And having them show up just when they did was probably the worst thing that could have happened to him.

I got to thinking about how bad he'd looked this morning. He must have put in a pretty rough day, so I decided I'd give him a break and have supper ready. I didn't think he'd be quite up to Kraft Dinner again, so I got real brave and tried bacon and eggs. The bacon part went okay, and about fifteen minutes before the time when he usually got home, I started the eggs. Eggs are tricky little critters. If you're not too experienced, it's pretty easy to get a little shell in there. I made some toast so there'd be something else crunchy and the eggshell wouldn't be quite so noticeable.

That was at a quarter to six. At six thirty I finally gave up and ate my share of the eggs. They reminded me a lot of inner tubes.

At seven I called Dad's boss to see if he was working late or something. He sounded surprised when I said Dad wasn't home yet. "Why, no, he's not here. He brought the county truck in at the usual time and left in his own truck. Maybe he had a flat tire or something."

Yeah, maybe, I thought. *Some flat that took over an hour to fix.*

I tried to study for the science test on Monday, but I couldn't concentrate. I've got too good an imagination, and it kept painting me pictures of gory accidents. Dad had been really tired. Maybe he went to sleep and . . .

When the phone rang, I literally jumped, hard enough to knock my science book on the floor. I was still shaking when I picked up the phone. I tried to control my voice when I said hello, but I guess I didn't do a very good job.

"Hi, Shane. You sound funny. What's the matter? Been out practicing cross-country some more?"

Casey.

"Oh, it's you," I blurted out, too worried to think about how disappointed I sounded.

"Well, excuse me! Who were you expecting? Olivia Newton-John?"

"Hey, don't get mad, Case," I said tiredly. "Dad hasn't showed up from work yet, and I don't know what's happened to him. I thought you might be him."

There was a pause. Then she said, "I'm sorry, Shane. I don't blame you for being worried. But give him a little more time. Anyway, what I phoned for was to see if you wanted to use my science notes to study all the stuff you missed earlier in the year. Why don't you come up here and we'll study together. Leave your dad a note to call you as soon as he gets home."

"Well, I don't know if . . ."

"Just a second, Shane. Mom's talking in my other ear." The line went silent for a minute. Then Mrs. Sutherland was speaking. "Listen, Shane. Casey just told me about your dad. I'm sure everything's okay and he's just been held up somewhere, so why don't you come up and study with Casey. Then, if he doesn't show up in an hour or so, we'll all go looking for him."

I didn't say anything.

"Come on. It's better than sitting there alone, imagining the worst."

She was right about that. "Yeah, okay. I'll be right up."

"Do you want me to pick you up?"

"No, I've got the bike. Thanks anyhow." I scribbled a note and left.

Casey and her mom and dad were sitting on the deck outside their living room. Their big German shepherd was lying beside Mrs. Sutherland, and a couple of fat cats were flaked out in the last of the sunshine. They all looked so much like the perfect family that someone should have written a grade one reader about them.

I went and sat down with them. Mrs. Sutherland started asking me questions about the Provincials tomorrow, and Casey started asking me if I knew what a euglena was. (I did, believe it or not.) The big tigery-looking cat came and hooked me in the leg till I picked him up and petted him. Mr. Sutherland just said hello and went back to studying some papers he had brought home with him to work on over the weekend. I wasn't sure why, but he and I seemed to make each other nervous. I don't think he could understand how Casey and her mother had got tangled up with a maverick like me, and to tell the truth, I couldn't understand how he fit in the same family with them. He sure wasn't like either one of them.

Before long Casey started asking me questions I couldn't answer, and I got so involved in trying to cram ten months of work into one night that I forgot all about the time.

When I looked at my watch again, it was nine o'clock.

Casey asked me another question, but I wasn't concentrating anymore. I was just going to try phoning home when I heard a car coming up the road, fast. The gravel crunched as the brakes grabbed and it turned into the driveway. It was Dad's truck. I breathed a sigh of relief. But I shouldn't have.

The truck didn't stop in the driveway. Dad drove it halfway across the lawn. Then I knew. Before he even got out of the truck, I knew.

He opened the door and almost fell out. Then he staggered over to the steps and grabbed the railing to keep from falling. I'd seen him drunk a lot of times. But never this drunk. He could hardly even talk.

"Hey, there, boy! What yu doin' up here when your old man's lookin' for yu? Come on. We gotta get home and pack your shtuff. We're hittin' the road."

I couldn't think. My mind felt the same way your jaw does when the dentist pumps it full of freezing. "What?" was all I could say.

Dad laughed, a crazy, drunken laugh. "You heard me. We're gettin' outta this dump. We don't need no stupid one-horse farm. Or that gut-bustin' grader ridin' either. We're goin' rodeoin'. I'm gonna be the champ again. So what yu waitin' for? Let's go!"

"No," I said.

Dad blinked. "What did you say?" he said slowly.

"I said I'm not going with you. Provincials are this weekend, and final exams are next week and . . ." I took a deep, shaky breath. I was so close to bawling, it wasn't funny, and I didn't much care what happened to me now. I didn't think anything could be worse than to have to stand here and watch Dad make a fool of himself in front of Casey and her parents. Especially her father. He was looking at Dad as if he was something that had just crawled out of a garbage can.

I kept talking. I knew I was going too far, but I couldn't get stopped. "And I've put too much into both of them to throw it all away and go trailing around after a washed-up has-been of a drunk bull rider!"

Dad must have moved awful fast for the shape he was in, or maybe I wasn't seeing too straight, but I never saw his hand move until it hit me square in the face. I fell backward against the railing, and a lot of things started happening all at once. But it seemed like they were in slow motion.

"Go in the house, Casey!" Mr. Sutherland yelled.

"No!" Casey yelled back.

"Stop it! All of you!" Mrs. Sutherland said, her voice low but furious.

"Shane, I didn't . . ." Dad muttered, looking at his hand like he was seeing it for the first time.

Then things were moving fast again. I was really bawling now, and I had trouble getting enough air to talk at the same time, but I managed to blurt out, "Go rodeoing! I don't care. Why didn't you just take off without me? It wouldn't be the first time you ran out on me. Anytime I've ever needed you, you haven't been there. So why change now? Why don't you just get out of my life? You don't care about me. You don't even care about yourself. The only person you ever really cared about was Mom. And you k—" Suddenly I realized what I was saying, and I almost choked on that word. I'd said a lot of terrible things, a lot more than I'd ever meant to say. And most of them had been true. But what I'd almost said just then scared me. That was one thing I could never say to Dad. No matter what he'd done, he didn't deserve that. Not when I knew that he must have said it to himself every day for four years. Not when I knew that he'd never stop blaming himself.

All the anger that had been blazing inside me a minute ago was suddenly gone. All that was left was a huge wave of shame that washed into me and took the anger's place. I looked up at Dad, towering above me. My big, tough, can-take-anything dad. . . .

But that wasn't true. Because the words I'd just thrown at him were something that Dad couldn't take. There was something terribly familiar in the helpless, haunted look that came across his face. *I didn't mean it,* I wanted to say. But I couldn't. I just stared back at him, trying to remember when I'd seen him look that way before. Then the chance to say it was gone, because, in a voice that had suddenly turned cold sober, Dad finished the sentence I'd cut off too late. "And I killed her. That's what you wanted to say, wasn't it, Shane? I guess you've been wantin' to say it for a long time."

Something in his voice touched a memory, and suddenly I knew when it was that I'd seen him look so hurt and confused before. That was the way he had been at the hospital, the night that Mom died.

It was like four years had just disappeared and we were back there again. It was like being in a nightmare I couldn't wake up from. And the worst part was that I was getting a sickening feeling that what he'd just said was too close to the truth. Maybe way deep down I had been blaming Dad for what had happened. Maybe I'd spent four years carrying that secret grudge, feeling it gnawing at my insides but never letting it out into the daylight 'cause I knew it was going to be too ugly to look at. Well, it was out now. It was out, but I wished to heaven that it wasn't. 'Cause getting it out of me wasn't worth laying it on Dad. I couldn't stand seeing that look on his face and knowing that this time I'd put it there.

I had to do something. I wanted to say something that would wipe out the last few minutes. But I couldn't. I couldn't explain to Dad. I was so mixed up, I couldn't even explain things to myself. I had to get out of there. . . .

Then I was running. Running blindly away from them all. I could hear someone yelling my name, but I didn't slow down. I jumped on the bike, and it started on the first try. My helmet was hanging on the handlebars, so I jammed it on my head to get it out of the way.

I didn't know where I was going, and I didn't care. I knew what I was leaving behind, and all I wanted was to get away just as far and as fast as that bike could take me.

17

I poured on every ounce of power that bike had. The faster, the better. Even if I didn't know where I was going, I wanted to get there in a hurry. The wind stung my bruised cheek, and a flash of anger swept over me at the thought of Dad hitting me like that. Then I thought about what I'd hit him with, and the guilty ache that swelled up in my throat hurt a lot worse than my face ever had. I didn't want to think anymore. Not yet, anyway. I tried to concentrate on the road, instead.

There's a curve just past the Sutherlands' place, with a low spot on the right shoulder that always fills up with rainwater and makes a big, gooey mud puddle. I remembered it just in time and swung wide around the curve to miss that mudhole. I swung a little too wide.

The car was green. It had a crack in the left headlight, and it was dirty. Time seemed to hang there for hours as those details imprinted themselves on my mind.

But really there was no time. Not even enough to get scared. *I'm going to hit*, I thought, almost calmly, and in that same split second I heard a sickening thump. I didn't feel anything. Or, if I did, I don't remember it.

I guess I was knocked out because I don't remember falling or anything. But I wasn't out for long because the next thing I knew, I heard a car door slam, and a lady I'd never seen before was running toward me, bawling her head off.

I wondered what she was crying about. She looked okay to me. But it was beginning to register that I probably wasn't okay. I still didn't feel anything, and that scared me worse than any amount of pain would have. I must have been in shock because my thinking was kind of irrational. I could taste blood, and I was sure that meant I'd knocked all my teeth out. All I could think of was that I'd have to go to the dentist, and that really upset me.

When it comes to dentists, I'm just pure chicken. I'm scared spitless of them. Always have been. I don't trust them. How do I know one of them won't let the drill slip and bore a hole in my lip or something? Then I saw that film *Marathon Man,* where the spies tortured the guy by drilling his teeth full of holes. It seemed all too believable to me.

The other thing that was really bothering me was that I was freezing cold—I read somewhere that you get cold when you're dying—and that scared me.

But finally I got my wits together enough to open my eyes again and really look the situation over. The good part of that was that I found out I wasn't necessarily feeling cold and clammy because I was dying. It was probably because I was lying right in the middle of the mudhole I'd been trying to miss.

The bad part was that I got a good look at my left leg, the one that had hit the front of the car. The angle of my foot alone would have been enough to tell me I'd busted the leg. Okay, I could accept that. People bust their legs every day. But then I took a closer look at my ankle and remembered that I wasn't wearing red socks. That was my leg. I caught a glimpse of a splinter of white bone sticking out. It looked just like the bone in Angel's leg.

I don't know if it was all the blood I'd swallowed or looking at the leg, but that's when I threw up.

The next few minutes are pretty confused in my mind. I don't remember seeing any more of the lady who hit me. I had a dim, panicky feeling that maybe she'd just run away and left me there. But I found out later that she'd just gone to the Sutherlands' to phone an ambulance.

I lost track of time in there, but it must have been only minutes later that the Sutherlands' van screeched to a stop at the edge of the road. When I opened my eyes, their whole family was there. Casey was crying. I wanted her to stop, but I couldn't think of anything to say to her. Her dad was looking even more worried than usual.

It's funny what really sticks in my mind about the whole scene. Even though I was only about half-conscious, what I do remember is still as clear as if I was watching it all flash by on television. And the part that I remember best was that Mrs. Sutherland was wearing her white pants. She waded out into that muddy water and got them all soaking wet and smeared up with mud and blood. I felt really bad about that, but I thought she should have known better than to wear white pants to an accident.

Then she was kneeling beside me, talking to me the same way she'd talked to Angel. She unbuckled my helmet and carefully lifted it off and set it on the ground. It was bright red, like the bike, and brand-new. But it didn't look new anymore. It was all muddy, like everything else. But even through the mud you could see the big dent in it and the scratches in the paint. I remembered that I'd almost thrown it away instead of jamming it on when I roared out of the yard. That bashed-in part would have been my head. I felt a little sicker, just thinking about it.

Mrs. Sutherland had her arm around me, and she was still talking. I don't remember a thing she said. I thought once she was crying, but I must have been wrong because she's not the crying kind. I was too sick and scared to care, just as long as she kept holding me.

But somewhere in the back of my mind I kept wondering where Dad was. He should have been there. There was some reason why he wasn't, but I couldn't remember what it was. I needed him. He should have been there.

I must have passed out for a while then because I remember opening my eyes and finding myself looking right at Dad. He was there. I was glad he was there, but for some reason I was kind of surprised to see him. He had a blanket in his hand, and he reached out and started to wrap it around me. *He's going to pick me up,* I thought, panicking. *No. Don't do that, Dad. Don't let anybody move me.* The first shock had worn off some, and now I was starting to hurt. As long as I lay perfectly still and didn't let myself think about it, the pain wasn't too bad. But I had a feeling that it was there, just out of reach, waiting to break loose if I let my guard down. Or if I moved, even a little. *No, Dad, please don't make me move. Just be here with me. That's all I need.* I wanted to say that to him. It was all planned that way in my head, but it was real hard to talk. I swallowed, shivering as I tasted blood again. "Don't touch me, Dad," I muttered thickly. Those were all the words I could get out. Then I started to cough, and I couldn't say anything for a minute. But I could see the look that came over Dad's face, and I remember thinking that he must have been in a lot more pain than I was right then. I had kind of a hazy feeling that maybe he and I weren't getting along very good, but I was too spaced out to remember why.

Then, before I could get it all figured out, his face suddenly sort of crumpled, and he turned and started to run toward the truck. I couldn't understand it at all. Why was he running away? It seemed like I'd been in this scene before somewhere. I just kept wondering what I'd said to make Dad run away from me. I noticed that he ran sort of funny. Maybe he'd been drinking. Maybe that was why he didn't understand.

I don't know how much time passed before the ambulance came. It seemed like forever, but I can't remember any more that happened in that time. I stayed sort of semiconscious. It was a weird feeling. As if I could bring myself fully awake if I really tried, but it was safer not to.

The next thing I really remember is catching a glimpse of a big gray building, and then a sign that said Emergency Entrance. Then someone flung open the doors, and we were in the hospital.

It was then that I started to panic. I'd known all along that I was hurt pretty bad, but I'd still been mostly in control, feeling I could handle whatever was happening to me. But now, inside the hospital, I was out of my territory. They could do whatever they wanted to me. And one thing for sure, they'd have to do something about that hunk of bone sticking out of my leg. And that meant surgery. They were going to put me to sleep.

I should have been glad. My leg was nearly killing me

now, and getting knocked out should have been the greatest thing that could happen to me. But there was something way back in my memory, something about waking up in a hospital. . . . If I could only think a little clearer, I'd remember what it was. They'd given me some kind of a shot on the way in. If it was supposed to be a pain-killer, it was doing a lousy job. What it was doing was fogging up my brain so I couldn't think straight, and the harder I tried to think of what was so bad about waking up in a hospital, the further away the answer seemed to get.

What I wished most was that these people would all get out and leave me alone. I felt rotten enough without them all flapping around me, cleaning me up, taking my blood pressure, putting on Band-Aids, and who knows what else. If an animal gets hurt, it just crawls into a quiet spot and either dies or gets better, alone. Animals aren't so dumb as they're made out to be.

I closed my eyes and tried to pretend I wasn't even there. I must have done a good job of it. The next thing I heard was these two guys, doctors, I guess, standing there talking about me like I was dead, or a hundred miles away.

"I thought he was scheduled for surgery right away."

"He is. But we're holding off a little, waiting to see if we can get parental consent."

"You mean the parents won't give it?"

"Parent. Singular. Mother's dead. The father hasn't showed up yet."

"Isn't he aware of the accident?"

"Oh, he's aware, all right. Apparently he and the kid had some sort of a run-in just before the kid took off and smacked his motorcycle head-on into a car. The father showed up at the scene of the accident just long enough to find out the kid was alive. Then he took off."

"Nice guy."

"Yeah. If you like drunks. The ambulance attendant said he was bombed out of his mind when he ran out on the kid."

Now I was remembering. I couldn't stop. But I didn't want to remember. I couldn't handle remembering.

I didn't know it was going to happen. I didn't mean to freak out like I did. One second I was lying there, half-conscious, and the next I was sitting up, screaming. "Stop it! Stop talking about me and do something! I can't take any more of this. Either let me out of here or give me something to knock me out! Just do something!"

If the orderly hadn't grabbed me, I think I'd have run out of that place, busted leg and all. But he was a big, strong guy, and even though he was real gentle with me, I didn't try sitting up again.

"Okay, we'll go without the consent. Get him ready. The kid's hurting too much to wait any longer."

He was right. But he didn't know anything about hurting. He thought it was just my leg.

I had another needle then, and this one really made me feel funny. "You'll be asleep in a minute," the nurse said.

Then that old, vague fear of waking up there swept back over me. "Don't wanna be asleep," I muttered.

A faraway voice said, "Let her talk to him. It might help."

Then someone squeezed my hand, and I looked up. A hazy outline of a woman's face was floating above me. She had blond hair, and she looked familiar. She was right there, brushing the hair out of my eyes with her cool hand, but her voice seemed to come from a long way off. "Take it easy, honey. It's going to be all right. I promise. Don't fight it. Just go to sleep."

"Mom? How'd you get . . . ?" I ran out of energy, and my voice trailed off into nothing.

"Shhh, don't talk. I'm here. That's all that matters." She squeezed my hand again, and I held on to her like she was all that was left in the world.

Darkness was wrapping itself around my mind, but I fought it off. There was something I had to tell her. Something really important. Suddenly I remembered.

"Mom," I said, but a whisper was all I could get out. She leaned closer to hear. "You've got to tell Dad I didn't mean it. . . ." There was more, but I couldn't find the words. The darkness was winning. I drifted deeper and deeper into the shadows until, at last, everything was just one big black shadow.

18

I woke up tired, confused, and hurting. Being unconscious ten hours hadn't changed things a whole lot. I made the mistake of opening my eyes, and a nurse pounced on me. "Well, good morning! And how's our boy today?" All sunshine and butterflies, that one. I wondered if she was a hallucination. I kind of hoped so. I gave her a dirty look and closed my eyes again.

The next time I woke up was a little better. I still wasn't feeling great, but I was thinking more clearly. I opened my eyes carefully; if that nurse was around, I was planning on playing possum. I was not in the mood for a chat.

No one was in sight, so I took a good look at the situation. The first thing I saw was my leg. It was hung in the air, attached to enough weights and cables to raise the *Titanic.* I guess they had the chunk of bone stuffed back into place anyway because everything was neat and tidy.

My left hand hurt, and when I went to move it, something really jabbed me. I turned my head and saw a tube sticking in my hand. Some colorless stuff was dripping down from a bottle on a stand. I looked like the star attraction on one of those medical shows.

My mouth was dry, and it tasted like a bear had been hibernating in it. I swallowed and ran my tongue over my teeth—my teeth! They were all there, after all! I wouldn't have to go to the dentist! Then I noticed that my bottom lip felt kind of fat. I touched it with my hand and wished I hadn't. It was stitched up like a quilt. So that was where all the blood had been coming from. Oh, well. Anything but teeth.

I sure wanted a drink. I thought about pushing the buzzer, but I was afraid Ol' Sunshine might come back. I'd wait.

It wasn't too long before a nurse showed up. It wasn't Sunshine. It was an older one who looked tired and kind of grumpy. "About time you were awake," she said. "I suppose you're thirsty?"

I nodded, and she handed me a glass with a bent straw. "Careful, you've got some stitches in your lip."

"I noticed," I croaked.

The juice helped. I sounded almost normal when I asked, "How long am I going to be in here?"

"Well, it's a bit soon to say. Why don't you just relax and concentrate on getting better."

Relax? Had she ever tried relaxing tied up like a calf at branding time?

I looked her right in the eye. "So give me a rough estimate. A week? Two?"

She sighed. "Don't count on it, son. If you're lucky, you might get out of traction in a month."

"A month?" I almost whispered it as I stared up at all that apparatus. Then a terrible thought hit me. "How do

I get out of all this stuff when I have to go to the bath-room?"

She smiled a wise and weary smile and said, "I'm afraid you don't."

Just then a cute redheaded candy striper came in, and that killed that conversation. I wasn't going any further on that subject with her there.

"Mrs. Redmond," she said to the nurse. "There's someone here to see Shane Morgan. Is he allowed company?"

Mrs. Redmond looked me over like she was trying to decide if I was going to survive. I didn't give her any encouragement. Nobody could survive a month with their leg tied to the ceiling.

"I'll check it out," she said, and they both left.

I wondered if it was Dad out there. No, it wouldn't be. He hadn't come last night, so why should I expect him today? But someone was here last night. I had the weirdest half-memory of it. . . .

Then the door opened, and Mrs. Sutherland came in. I don't know why, but I almost started bawling when I saw her. She sat down beside me. "Well, Tiger, you look better than you did last night."

I tried to grin and jumped at the pain that shot through my lip.

She put her hand on my arm. "Easy, Shane. Just lie still and listen, okay? I talked to the doctor. He says it's a pretty bad break, but he thinks it should heal as good as ever."

"Yeah! After a month or more of being tied up in this!" I said furiously, glaring at all the stuff around me.

Mrs. Sutherland stopped smiling. She was dead serious when she said, "If you only knew how lucky you are to have a leg to tie up."

That shut me up for a minute. But there was one question I had to ask, even though I didn't think I wanted to hear the answer. "Where's Dad?" I said.

I'd never known Mrs. Sutherland not to be able to look you in the eye when she told you something. But now she looked down and wound her watch as she answered so low I could hardly hear her. "I don't know. He hasn't come home since the accident." She looked up and saw the look on my face. "Listen, Shane, I know how it must seem to you, but try to understand how . . ."

I turned my face into the pillow. "My leg's hurting. Just leave me alone."

She sighed and was quiet for a long time. Then she stood up. "Okay, if that's the way you want it. It's time I was getting home anyway."

I hadn't meant to hurt her feelings. Jeff had sure been right about me not being much good at untangling things. All I did was make a worse mess. Then I looked up into her face, and I knew what I'd been half-remembering about last night. "Hey," I said, "I'm sorry I kept calling you Mom last night."

She gave me a funny look, and her voice sounded kind of hoarse when she answered. "Don't be sorry, Shane. I'm not." Suddenly she bent over and kissed my cheek.

Then she was gone. And that hospital turned into the lonesomest place in the world. I didn't go to sleep for a long time. My leg was hurting a lot. The nurse had said I could have a shot of pain-killer if I wanted, but that stuff they'd given me last night had mixed me up so bad that I'd rather have the pain.

I lay there staring at the date on a chart that the night-light was shining on. June 16. That date meant something. Cross-country Provincials. I should have been running in Edmonton today. And for the first time I realized that no matter what I'd told myself, I really had wanted to run in Provincials, a lot.

Casey came to see me the next day. I think she was half-scared to come because she sent her mom in first to ask me if I wanted to see her. For the smartest girl in class she sure could be dumb. Just because I was mad at the whole world didn't mean I was mad at her. Or her mom.

Mrs. Sutherland left to do some shopping and sent Casey in. She stopped about ten feet from the bed, and we stared at each other. I was kind of embarrassed, lying there with my bare leg in the air and everything, and Casey didn't seem to know how to handle the situation either.

"Hi," she said in a small voice.

"Hi," I said.

We stared at each other some more. "So . . . uh . . . how are you—" she started, but I didn't give her a chance to finish. I had been asked that question at least a hundred times that day, and she was the first person I knew well enough to get mad at.

"Case! If you ask me how I'm feeling, I'm going to throw you out of here!"

She gave me a strange look, probably trying to decide if I'd suffered brain damage. Then she started to smile, and the smile turned into a giggle. "You sure don't look as dangerous as you sound," she said.

I wasn't in the mood to find anything funny, especially not myself, but looking at her, I suddenly found myself grinning. I also found myself getting a kink in my neck trying to see her at all. "Hey," I said. "It's not contagious, you know."

"What?" she said, giving me that puzzled look again.

"The busted leg. Are you just going to stand there waiting for me to get up, or are you going to come over here and talk to me?"

She came and sat by the bed and looked over all the junk I was hung up in. "Yuk, that is gross! Does it hurt?"

"Some."

We kept running out of things to say to each other. Probably because we were avoiding the things that really needed saying. Finally I had to get it over with. "Listen, Casey, about Friday night. I'm sorry I got into that fight with Dad at your place."

"It wasn't your fault that he was drunk."

"Yeah, but I didn't have to pick a fight with him in front of your whole family."

She gave me a long look then, and somehow it made me feel like I was a lot younger than her. "Shane," she said in kind of a tired voice, as if she was explaining something to a slow learner, "I wish you'd quit thinking that just because we live in that big 'castle' on the hill, it's the Sutherland Magic Kingdom, where the rain never falls. I mean, I wasn't going to faint dead away because you and your dad did a little yelling at each other. Don't you think I've seen a family fight before?"

That was one of those questions that there is no safe answer to. "Well, I mean, your family would never . . ." I had the sentence started, but I couldn't figure out how it was going to end. Casey interrupted and saved me the trouble anyway.

She shook her head. "Get serious, Shane. You've seen

enough of my parents to know how different they are
from each other. Don't you think they ever see things
differently? Don't you think they ever get mad at each
other?"

This time I had sense enough not to try to think of an
answer.

"I'd bet you a lot of money that when it comes right
down to it, our family doesn't get along any better than
you and your dad do."

I thought that over. Maybe there was some truth to
that. My mind went back to the night in the Sutherlands'
yard. In between all the yelling Dad and I did, it seemed
to me that they had done some yelling, too.

"Yeah, Case, I see what you mean. But there's one big
difference."

"What's that?"

"You never said anything so bad to your dad that he
couldn't come back."

"Your dad knows you didn't mean those things."

"Yeah? Then how come he's gone? How come he just
left me lying there on the road and never even came to
the hospital?"

I didn't really expect that she had an answer, but what I
got was a question.

"Why'd you get on that motorcycle and tear out of our
place that night, Shane?"

I didn't like that question. I liked the answer even less.
I stared at the ceiling. " 'Cause I couldn't take any more
of what was happening between Dad and me."

I had a feeling Casey had just proved a point, but she
kept talking anyway. "And if your fast trip to nowhere
hadn't got messed up by a car, were you planning to just
keep running forever?"

It was beginning to feel like I was being interrogated by the RCMP. "No," I muttered. "I would've come back after I got things straightened out a little better."

Casey nodded. "You and your dad aren't as different as you think," she said.

"What's that supposed to mean?"

She just grinned. "He'll be back," she said, like she knew what she was talking about.

I wanted to believe it, but I didn't know what to believe anymore. I just didn't know.

19

I was asleep on Monday afternoon when the nurse came to ask if I wanted to see one of my friends from school. I didn't know who it could be, but I could hardly say no.

I almost fell out of bed when Bart Willard walked in. He was about the last person I expected to see, or wanted to see, for that matter. He was carrying a huge trophy under his arm and looking about as out of place in a hospital as a bull at a dinner party. He looked me over and shook his head. "Morgan, you are a mess," he said. Well, I couldn't argue with that, but coming from him, I didn't like it any too much. While I was trying to decide what to say he set the trophy on the table. "We won the Provincials. Since you were on the team, the coach thought you should see the trophy."

He did? Now that was hard to take in. "Nice trophy," I said, with about as much enthusiasm as I felt. I guess I was kind of glad for the team, but Bart was not the person to send if they wanted to spread sunshine to the sick.

Then, since I was already in the hospital, I couldn't

resist ruffling old Bart's fur a little. "How's Cheryl?" I asked innocently. "Did she win her race?"

He gave me a look that could have peeled paint. "Yeah, she won. What's it to you, Morgan?"

I smiled up at him. "Nothing. I just wondered how she was doing."

He glared at me for a few seconds more. Then he turned and slouched toward the door. Either his two-minute attention span had run out, or talking about Cheryl made him feel kind of uncomfortable. I figured that if he was going to keep hanging around her, he might just as well get used to that feeling. One evening with her made me feel uncomfortable enough to last a lifetime.

"Yeah, well, stay outta trouble, Morgan," Bart said as he started out the door.

"Hey, what about the trophy?" I yelled after him.

"Aw, keep it here. You're the only one that's got time to look at it." Then he was gone. I spent the rest of the afternoon trying to figure out what that little visit had been all about.

That night, when Mrs. Sutherland came to see me, she brought a surprise, too. A big pair of scissors that she dug out of the depths of her purse. They were dangerous-looking things. I was sure I'd seen them in the operating room of her clinic.

"Okay," she said. "Close your eyes, don't move, and it won't hurt much." She gave me a very complete haircut. When I saw the amount of hair she threw in the garbage, I was afraid I was going to have to become a punk rocker. But she seemed to think she'd done a great job.

"Hey," I said. "Where'd you learn to cut hair?"

She shrugged. "Well, I never really tried a human before, but I've trimmed a lot of horses' tails, and hair is hair. You look much better."

After she left, I got up nerve enough to look in the mirror. I should've gone for the pink ribbon instead of the haircut.

Speaking of the pink ribbon, Miss Bradley came to see me on the last day of school. She looked a little worn around the edges as she flopped down in a chair. "Don't ask me what I'm doing here! Only creeping insanity would make me want to see one more kid today. . . . Hey!" she interrupted herself. "You got your hair cut!" Then she took a closer look and added, "I think. Or was that part of the damage from the accident?"

Okay, I owed her one. I made a mental note of a garter snake for her desk drawer next fall.

Then she got serious. "Anyway, I'm glad you're going to be okay. We've missed you. The class has been almost disgustingly quiet without you! And about your exams— all the teachers talked it over and decided that from what we'd seen of your work, you'd have done all right on them. So you're officially in grade nine." She was going to say something else when she happened to turn and see that trophy sitting there. "Where did that come from?" she asked, all excited.

"Bart brought it to show me, right after the Provincials. Don't ask me why. He said the coach sent him with it."

Miss Bradley started to laugh. "Bart said the coach sent it? The coach has been turning the school over for a week, trying to find it! He thinks somebody stole it. If he knew it had been in the hospital all the time . . ."

"I think you'd better take it with you," I said. Even though I had passed all my other subjects, I'd just thought of a surefire way to flunk phys. ed. if I wasn't careful. Trust good ol' Bart.

I was still laughing to myself over that trophy when this strange, dressed-up lady walked in. I didn't know it, but she was about to drop a bombshell that would sober me up real fast.

She walked right up, all cool, like she owned the place, and said, "Hello, Shane, my name is Sheila Patterson." Instantly, and unreasonably, I hated her. Five minutes later I'd still be hating her, but by then I'd have a reason.

Now she sat down beside the bed and went on, "I'm a social worker, and I've been assigned to you, so I'd like to ask you a few questions." Her smile was so phony-sweet that if she'd been outside, she'd have attracted every wasp in the country.

What did I need with a social worker? I didn't even know what they did. Something to do with getting on welfare and stuff like that, I thought. Well, we might not have much money, but we always got by . . . at least when Dad was here. Suddenly the pieces started falling into place, and I started to panic. Dad wasn't here—that was why she was here. I got a terrible hollow feeling in the pit of my stomach.

I knew how Dad would have handled Sheila Patterson. He'd have told her to take her questions and . . . get lost. So why couldn't I do that? Because I was just a kid. And kids aren't supposed to fight back. They're supposed to be polite and do what they're told, even when they know it's all a setup. I stared at the ceiling while she got out her notebook and started asking her questions.

She started with the basic stuff. My age, birthplace, parents' names. Then she stopped playing around and got down to what she really wanted to know about.

"How long has your mother been dead, Shane?"

Leave me alone, lady. You can't walk in here and start asking me questions like that. I wished I had the guts to say it out loud. But I didn't say anything.

"How long, Shane?" she repeated, her voice still sweet but with a little hard core underneath.

"Four years," I muttered.

"And your father has taken care of you during that time?"

"Yeah."

"You and your father have just moved to the Deer Valley area. Where did you live before that?"

In our half-ton. On the road, between rodeos. How do you like that one, lady? "A lot of places," I said carefully.

"What about school? Did you stay in one place long enough to attend the same school for a whole term?"

I shook my head, and she wrote in her book.

She sort of cleared her throat before she tried the next question. She was having trouble finding a nice way to say it. "Shane, your father, uh, seems to have a drinking problem. We'd like to help him with it if he needs help. Maybe you can give us some information on that. Is it true? In your opinion, is his drinking out of control?"

I looked at her, sitting there in her expensive suit and fingernail polish. And I thought, *I hit Bart Willard for saying the same thing you're trying to say. Who makes the rules that say you can get away with saying it?*

"No, it isn't true," I said, looking her right in the eye and lying through my teeth. "My dad's okay," I said and suddenly realized that I wasn't lying about that part. I meant it.

She wrote a lot about that one. I watched her and noticed that she didn't look quite as confident as she had when she started. I knew she was just trying to do her job, and I wasn't making it easy for her. But she wasn't exactly making it easy for me either.

"Where is your father now, Shane?" she asked, and I died inside. I didn't say anything.

"Do you know where he is?"

"No," I whispered. *There it is, lady. You got it all. Write it down in your book. One abandoned kid to dispose of.*

But she still wasn't finished with me. "When you are released from the hospital, you will have to have somewhere to go. Do you have any relatives you could stay with?"

I shook my head, and she wrote some more. Then she closed the book, smiled her professional smile, and came out with the prize-winning line of the year. "Don't worry, Shane. We'll arrange for a temporary foster home for you until we can work out something. Everything will be fine." She gathered up her stuff and walked away.

Don't worry? And in the same breath, we'll put you in a foster home! The words *foster home* got trapped in my head and kept echoing around there. Foster homes were for orphans. And I wasn't an orphan. I had a father, somewhere. Or were they for kids whose parents never wanted to see them again?

I wished I hadn't bothered putting my helmet on before I took off on the bike. I might be dead now.

An hour later Casey came charging in, wearing dirty blue jeans and a torn sweat shirt and talking in overdrive from the minute she opened the door. "Hey, Shane! Guess what! Mom and I went to check on Angel today. And when the horses saw the oats, they all came galloping toward us. And Angel was in front. In front! Running flat out! Hardly limping at all! Mom says it looks like there won't be any permanent damage. Just a scar. And it's not so bad living with a scar . . ."

She finally ran out of breath and slowed down enough to look at me. Her smile faded, and she said in a real low voice, "What's wrong, Shane?"

"Case, just go away, please. I don't feel like talking right now." I turned to face the wall and closed my eyes. I hoped she'd think I was sick. I really did feel sick.

She didn't leave. Even with my eyes closed, I could feel her staring at me. Finally I couldn't stand it any longer, and I turned over and looked at her. There were tears on her cheeks. I felt worse than ever. I didn't mean to hurt her, of all people.

She swallowed hard. "You just about chased me into the beaver dam once, to find out why I wasn't talking. There's no place to chase you to."

I didn't say anything.

Angrily she wiped her sleeve across her eyes. "Look, you stupid jerk. In case you hadn't noticed, I care what happens to you. Now, what's wrong?"

Getting started talking was the hard part. But once I started, I couldn't get stopped. Somewhere in the middle of the story Mrs. Sutherland came in, but I kept going.

I held together right until the end. But when I got to ". . . and so they're going to put me in a foster home . . ." my voice broke. *Foster home* might as well have been *electric chair.* It had the same effect on me.

Then Casey started crying again, too, and the next thing I knew, her mom was sitting on the edge of the bed with an arm around each of us. "Okay, okay," she said softly. "It's all right. Everything's all worked out. This just came in the mail." She held out an envelope.

I didn't know what she was talking about, but I took it.

My hand started shaking when I recognized the writing. I pulled out the letter and read.

Dear Mrs. Sutherland,

There's nothing I can say that would tell you how bad I feel about my behavior the night of the accident. I know I am to blame for everything, and I'm really sorry about it all.

I guess Shane thinks I ran out on him again, and I can't deny that I did. But I hope he doesn't think it was his fault. It wasn't. All the things he said were true, and it was about time somebody finally said them. Now maybe we can finally bury them.

I don't really understand why I ran off that night. Except that I seem to be real good at running when the going gets tough. I guess it was mostly that I was feeling so guilty about everything, and knowing the way Shane was feeling about me right then, it seemed like getting out of there was the best thing I could do for him. That, and the fact that I was still so drunk I couldn't think straight at all.

But I've done a lot of thinking since then. Every time I close my eyes, I can see him lying there on the road. I came so close to losing him. But maybe that's what it took to make me realize how much that kid means to me. He's the one thing I've got in this world that's worth fighting for.

I know I've got an awful lot to make up for, and it's not going to be easy. But I've quit drinking. And I'm working now, so I'm sending you a check to cover Shane's board. I hope it's not asking too much of you to look after him for me. I got the feeling that you liked him, and I know he thinks the world of you.

I don't know when I'll be back. I think Shane needs some time, and I'm not sure I'm ready to face him yet. But when I come back, it'll be for good. That's a promise.

I don't have a permanent address, so there's no point in writing back, but I'll be in touch.

Thanks for everything.

Josh Morgan

P.S. If you think he's ready to hear it, tell Shane I'm sorry. And I miss him.

There was a check for two hundred dollars in the envelope, and the letter had been postmarked in Wyoming.

That was an awful lot of writing for Dad, and I had trouble taking it all in. But I understood one thing. Dad was coming back. And that was all that really mattered.

I handed the letter back to Mrs. Sutherland. "I stopped and saw the social worker on my way in," she said. "Do you think you could stand the idea of a foster home if it was our place?"

I didn't trust myself to talk just then, so I nodded. It looked like Mrs. Sutherland had just collected another stray.

20

Four days after they took the cast off, I walked out of the hospital—on crutches, that is. But I didn't care about that. I would have crawled if it had meant getting out.

Living at the Sutherlands' was like being part of a real family again. Mrs. Sutherland spoiled me rotten, and Casey even forgot herself and waited on me sometimes. I was sure they'd both get over it as soon as I started walking a little better, but I made the most of it while it lasted.

Actually the next week Casey forgot all about looking after me. She'd managed to talk her parents into letting her race Blue at the Deer Valley Rodeo, and from then on she had a one-track mind. The way she was training that horse, you would have thought that "under sixteen" race was the Kentucky Derby.

I had Reb up at the Sutherlands' with me, and I'd have given my front teeth to race him, too, but the doctor had said, "Absolutely no riding for at least another month."

I didn't cheat until the day before the rodeo. Then I just couldn't help it. Blue really needed one good run against another horse. Casey had to admit that it was true, so we saddled Reb and sneaked him out the back door of the barn. I couldn't put my left foot in the stirrup, so I had to get on from the right side, but with Casey holding Reb it worked okay. It felt good to be on a horse again! And as long as I didn't try putting my foot in the stirrup, it didn't even hurt.

We raced the quarter mile of trail between the beaver dam and the woods. It was close all the way, but at the end Blue pulled ahead by a couple of lengths. I was glad for Casey because it gave her confidence for the race the next day. But I told Reb that he'd have won for sure if I hadn't been riding off-balance. He agreed.

We were heading back along the woods trail when we came around a corner and ran smack-dab into Mrs. Sutherland, riding out to check on some cattle.

That was the first time I'd ever been yelled at by her. And I wouldn't want to make it a habit. She was some steamed up!

"Shane! You empty-headed twit! You want to see the instant replay of that month in traction, you just keep messing around until you break that leg again!"

Well, there are times when you might as well keep your mouth shut and take it. I knew this was one of them. But Casey didn't. "But, Mom, he was just racing Reb against Blue so we could see how . . ."

"I don't care if he was practicing for the world-champion-idiot contest! And you, hotshot jockey that you've become, no doubt talked him into it! Now, you two get home! And supper had better be on the table by the time I get there." She nudged her horse ahead and then reined him in. "Well," she said, "since you did it, you might as well tell me who won."

"Blue. By two lengths," Casey said.

Her mother nodded. "Good!" Then she pulled her hat down and galloped off.

Casey and I just sat there in the settling dust for a minute. Then we looked at each other. I don't know which of us got the wicked idea first, but suddenly we were both grinning. I gathered up my reins. "To the barn!" I yelled and leaned low over Reb's neck. We were off like a bullet, Casey and Blue right beside us.

Neck and neck, our horses slid to a stop by the barn door with Casey and me both laughing so hard we couldn't talk. My leg was hurting something fierce, but I felt great!

Morning seemed to come early the next day with everybody running around getting organized for the Deer Valley Rodeo. I hadn't been to a rodeo for a long time, and I should have been looking forward to going to this one. I wasn't really, though. Partly I suppose it was because I was feeling kind of sorry for myself limping around on crutches while Casey had all the fun.

But the main reason was that I'd never been to a rodeo that Dad wasn't going to be in. It just didn't feel right without him.

We unloaded Blue back behind the chutes, and then Mr. Sutherland parked right up close to the arena fence where we could get a good look at the action in the chutes.

Deer Valley didn't have the world's best-organized rodeo. It was late starting, and when the first event, the bareback, finally did get started, there were a lot of long pauses between rides. They seemed to have a lot of trouble getting the stock into the chutes, and from the looks of the fence around the arena I figured the whole layout could use some rebuilding.

Then it was time for Casey's race, and we watched as seven or eight horses paraded in front of the grandstand. They were a real mixture. A couple of local kids' ponies, fat and soft, and obviously just brought out of the pasture. No threat. Then there were two big Thoroughbred-looking ones, with racing saddles and all. Mr. Sutherland took one look at them and groaned to himself, but I didn't think he needed to worry. On a big track in a long race maybe, but not in a quarter mile. But there was an Indian kid with a lean, hard-muscled bay. That one I'd watch. And a little sorrel barrel-racing horse. She had some short-distance speed.

Then they were lining up. No starting gates at these little rodeos, just a starter who lines them up the best he can and then fires the gun.

They were off! The Indian kid was ahead. You could see that he'd been in a lot of these races, and he hadn't lost any time. Maybe he'd even jumped the gun a little, but I couldn't be sure.

Blue and the sorrel were next, right together, and the rest of the field spread out behind. I'd been right about the Thoroughbreds. They couldn't handle that kind of a start. One reared and almost threw his rider, and the other froze for a second, probably wondering when the gate was going to open.

Halfway around, Blue was pulling away from the sorrel. He had the speed to beat that horse, but I wasn't so sure about the bay. A hundred yards left, and the bay was still three lengths ahead. Then suddenly the Thoroughbred that had started so slow was passing the sorrel and coming up fast on Blue. For some reason that big horse must have scared the daylights out of the little roan because I saw him turn his head a little to see what was coming. That was all he needed. Suddenly he was passing that bay like it was trotting, and he was still adding daylight between him and the Thoroughbred when he crossed the finish line.

When Casey got back to us, she had a trophy, a twenty-dollar check, and a huge grin to go with them. She was so excited that we heard the instant replay of that race ten times in a row. Finally her dad looked at her mom and sighed. Mrs. Sutherland winked at him. I knew what they were thinking. Give the kid one chance to race and what happens? She wins. And they've got an addict on their hands. Actually I couldn't blame Casey. Not when I remembered the first time I'd won a steer-riding buckle. I'd even taken Mom and Dad out to dinner (at McDonald's, of course) on the prize money.

Then it was time for the bull riding, and I felt myself go tense. Even though Dad wouldn't be in it this time, I couldn't just turn off all those years of being proud and scared and excited, all mixed together. It was a habit.

This stock contractor had some rank bulls. We watched them as they trotted down the alley from the holding pens to the chutes, snorting and bellowing and challenging the world to fight.

Then the clown came trotting into the arena. He'd spent a lot more time on his makeup than a lot of them did. His face was really painted up. He had on baggy overalls and the brightest blaze-orange shirt I'd ever seen, topped off by a long red and white polka-dot scarf around his neck. If that getup didn't get the bulls' attention, nothing would.

He bowed to the main grandstand, then turned

around and looked right at us. And for a second I
stopped breathing. He looked so much like . . . It
could be. He had said he was coming back. Clowns
worked whatever rodeo they wanted to. There was no
reason he couldn't be at this rodeo. . . . I stopped myself. It was stupid getting my hopes up like that. Wishful
thinking can do funny things to your imagination. This
was just another clown.

There were some good riders here, a few I knew by
sight, but none of Dad's friends. I guess this rodeo wasn't
big enough to pay traveling expenses from very far. Anyway, I was glad they weren't here. I wouldn't have known
what to say to them anymore.

Most of the bulls seemed to be coming out ahead of
the riders, but the action was great. Casey had managed
to come down to earth enough to lean on the front
bumper of the van, and her dad was watching from the
front seat. I was sitting in front of the van, feeling like
someone's granny on the lawn chair they'd insisted on
bringing for me. Mrs. Sutherland had been sitting beside
me, but one of the local calf ropers had come and asked
her to look at a cut on his horse's leg. I could see she
didn't want to miss the bull riding, but she had gone. It
was part of the job.

They were having trouble with the bull in the nearest
chute. He was out to wreck everything he could reach.
That rider must have been down on him ten times, but
every time the bull started tearing around and hooking
back at his legs, so he had to get off again. I could imag-
ine what that guy was feeling like. A bull like that could
kill you. He'd tear you apart before he ever got you out of
the chute. And if he couldn't do it physically, he'd do it

mentally. He'd psych you out, get you so rattled that he had the advantage.

That's just what this bull did. Suddenly the rider was down on him again and nodding to the gate man to let them out. He hadn't been ready; he just couldn't stand the waiting.

He lasted two jumps before the bull spun him off. He landed to the side and a little behind, a good place to come off a bull. And he was lucky. His hand jerked loose right away. If you got hung up on a bull like that one . . .

The clown was good. He was right there, between the cowboy and the bull, giving the rider the seconds he needed to get out of there. The bull hesitated, pawing the ground and looking as if he might go for the clown. Then something happened to change his mind. Suddenly, out of nowhere, a little white poodle came tearing out from under the Sutherlands' van, yapping his fool head off. The bull forgot the clown, and all the smoldering hate in his eyes focused on that hyperactive scrap of fur. He charged. The dog stuck his tail between his legs and scrambled back under the van, yapping all the way.

The bull didn't even slow down for the fence. I don't think a new one would have held him, and this one was anything but new. When he hit, the post snapped with the sound of a rifle shot. There was a screech of tearing wire, and the single gasp of a thousand spectators as they saw what was happening.

Then an eerie almost-silence fell as the bull paused for a second in what was left of the fence. He pawed the ground. I could hear his breathing, that rough, out-of-his-mind-furious breathing that means a bull is mad enough to smash the nearest thing he can get at.

And the nearest thing was me. My crutches were on

the ground beside me, and I knew there was no way I could get out of there fast enough. It was just like when I smashed up the bike. I could see it coming. I knew it was going to happen. But I couldn't move. All I could do was wait for it.

All at once a streak of blaze-orange flashed across the corner of the arena. The clown. Trying to turn the bull. That was what he got paid for, getting it to go for him instead. But there wasn't time. The bull was too close. He lowered that huge head and blew through his nostrils, and I could feel the hot air on my face. He pawed once more and started coming.

But the clown was close now, with that huge polka-dot scarf in his hand. For a split second he turned and looked at me, and his eyes, those Morgan-blue eyes, met mine. "Dad!" I yelled. It really was him. And this time he wasn't running away. He was running as hard as he could straight toward me and toward the bull.

Then he was between the bull and me. He turned and his hand flashed out, flicking the scarf across the bull's face, the same way a matador would use his cape, attracting all that fury to himself. And with unbelievable coordination a ton of Brahma swerved and lunged after its new enemy. One powerful shoulder sideswiped me and knocked me over, but that was all.

I looked up just in time to see the bull toss his head, hooking in a half-circle with his horns. They caught Dad and threw him high in the air. He landed face-down in the dirt of the arena.

There were half a dozen pick-up men around that bull then. Ropes settled around his neck from two directions, and they dragged him out of there.

I didn't care about the bull. I don't know if I ran or

crawled or flew, but the next thing I knew, I was out there in the dirt, beside Dad.

I'd been scared before, but never in my life had I been as scared as I was when I reached out and turned him over.

The bull's horn had torn his shirt open and left a long bloody scratch across his chest. Outside of that there wasn't a mark on him. He just lay there with his eyes closed not moving.

Oh, God! Don't let him be dead! Not now. Not now that I know how much I need him.

Somewhere along the way I started saying the words out loud. "You can't die! I need you. I love you, Dad." I wondered when I had said that last. It had been a long, long time ago. Now I suddenly realized that I'd never stopped meaning it. At last, when it might be too late, I could say it.

His eyes flickered open, blinked a couple of times, and finally focused on me. "Quit yellin' in my ear, Shane. I ain't dead."

Then he was sitting up. Sitting in the middle of the arena, in front of everybody, hugging me so tight I couldn't breathe. Hugging me and crying all over his makeup. Josh Morgan was crying! "I love you too, kid," he whispered.

A thousand people in the grandstand were standing up, clapping, as we helped each other up and limped out of the arena.

When us Morgans fight, half the world knows it. When we make up, the whole world knows it. And we'd had about enough of fighting. We were ready to start trying to do some untangling.

EPILOGUE

It was the last day of summer holidays. The last day of the worst-best summer of my life, and I was trying to sleep in one last time. But Dad dragged me out of bed at daylight. "Come on," he said. "There's something for you out here."

We headed for the barn, and for a minute I was afraid he had another motorcycle stashed out there. It wasn't a motorcycle.

It was Angel, standing there bridled and wearing my saddle. "She's healed up good enough to start working. And you're healed up good enough to start riding her," Dad said slowly. Then as he handed me the reins he added, "And I guess I'm finally healed up enough to know that there's nothin' your mom would have liked better than for you to have her horse."

FAR FROM HOME
Ouida Sebestyen

Salty had promised his dying mother that he would keep the family together—no matter what.

An orphan at 13, Salty is left to take care of his great grandmother. Facing homelessness and starvation during the Great Depression, he seeks work and shelter at the Buckley Arms, where his mother worked until her death. Once there, discovering the link between his mother and Tom Buckley becomes of vital importance to Salty.

LAUREL-LEAF BOOKS $2.95 92640-8-28